*A
Harlequin
Romance*

OTHER
Harlequin Romances
by MARY WIBBERLEY

Many of these titles are available at your local bookseller
or through the Harlequin Reader Service.

For a free catalogue listing all available Harlequin Romances,
send your name and address to:

HARLEQUIN READER SERVICE,
M.P.O. Box 707, Niagara Falls, N.Y. 14302
Canadian address: Stratford, Ontario, Canada N5A 6W4

or use order coupon at back of book.

THE DARK ISLE

by

MARY WIBBERLEY

HARLEQUIN BOOKS   TORONTO
WINNIPEG

Harlequin edition published November 1975

SBN 373-01924-6

Original hard cover edition published in 1975
by Mills & Boon Limited.

*All the characters in this book have no existence outside the
imagination of the Author, and have no relation whatsoever to
anyone bearing the same name or names. They are not even
distantly inspired by any individual known or unknown to the
Author, and all the incidents are pure invention.*

Printed in Canada

1924

CHAPTER ONE

'COME home,' the telegram said, 'Daddy gone mad.' And as if that were not sufficiently dramatic, it finished: 'Most urgent.'

Janis Sutherland took a deep breath and counted to ten. Very slowly. Allowing for her sisters' wild exaggeration, there was something clearly amiss, and she had to know what it was as soon as possible.

'What does it say, Jan?' her aunt Ina called from the kitchen.

Janis closed the front door of her aunt's flat and crossed the hall. 'It looks as though Dad's up to something again,' she said. 'Can I phone home?'

'Of course, my dear. He's not ill, is he?'

Jan was already on her way back to the hall. 'I doubt it,' she called. 'They just said he'd gone mad.'

'Oh *dear*,' Aunt Ina's sigh said more than her words.

There was no S.T.D. on Dark Isle. Nothing so simple as dialling your number and being immediately connected. Jan stared at herself in the mirror by the phone and wondered why it was that she couldn't even come for a few quiet days' shopping in Edinburgh without Craigie House falling apart in her absence. Wide dark eyes stared back at her, and she wrinkled her nose at her reflection and wondered if she would ever be beautiful, like Diane was. A little sigh escaped her, abruptly stopped as the operator's voice came in a helpful burr:

'Numberrr, *please*.'

No wonder Judy and Helen had sent a telegram. The process of getting through on the phone involved minutes of complicated and technical sounding whirrs and clicks and pips, interrupted by an occasional: 'I am trying to connect you—hold the line, *please*.'

Jan sighed. She knew she shouldn't grumble. Let everywhere else be civilized and up to date, but Dark Isle would never—*must* never change, because it was perfect as it was, a tiny place that the world had forgotten—if indeed it had ever known about it. One village, three shops, one inn, mail twice a week, and the only industries knitting and fishing, and everything idyllic.

But—just once—Jan thought it might have been nice to get through on the phone without a twenty-minute wait during which time all sorts of dire possibilities occurred to her about her father's mental stage . . .

'Here you are, love,' a cup was placed beside her, and Aunt Ina smiled reassuringly. 'Don't worry. You know what those two sisters of yours are like——'

'I do,' Jan smiled at her aunt in reply. The mirror into which she had so recently been glancing captured the smile, and showed the beauty of it, but Jan wasn't looking. It was only rarely that she considered her looks, and she was too busy concentrating on the task in hand to look into the glass again. Only fleetingly, when she thought of Diane, the eldest of the four sisters, who now lived in London and was married to someone in TV—and she had only thought of her a few moments ago because there was a copy of the *Radio Times* on the telephone table, and it had jogged her memory. Television! Jan looked down and picked up the cup of tea. How anyone in their right mind could go and work for that——

'Oh! Hello!' The clicks and whirrs changed tone, and a sound emerged from the miles of wires and said in a very timid voice:

'Craigie House.'

'Judy? It's me, Jan.'

'Jan! Oh, *Jan*!' Even across the miles the relief flowed out of the telephone in waves. 'You got the telegram?'

'Yes, love, and that's why I'm phoning. What is it? What has happened?'

'It's Daddy—there's this man—and he—oh, it's awful——'

'Stop!' Jan said firmly. 'What man? Begin at the beginning.'

'Yesterday a man arrived at the house and said he'd come to see Daddy and——' her voice faded, and Jan said impatiently:

'What is it?'

'I can't *talk* now—he's just come in,' her sister's muffled but urgent words came back. 'Just come home. He's very big and——' a pause. 'That's better, he's gone out again. He and Daddy are as thick as thieves—oh, Jan, never mind buying curtains and all that stuff, just come back, you *know* you're the only one who can deal with Daddy—they keep going out for walks—and *looking at the house*——'

'I'm on my way,' Jan answered grimly. 'Don't worry. I'm getting the next train back.' She put the phone down, too agitated to realize she had not said goodbye.

'Sorted out?' Her aunt was waiting near her. Jan

took a swallow of hot tea.

'I'll have to go. I don't know what he's up to, but I've got a damned good idea. This strange man has arrived, and Dad and he keep having looks round the house, and long walks——'

'Oh no, he's not thinking of selling again?'

'Over my dead body! And that's why I've got to go.' Jan went to hug her aunt. 'You know what it means to me, don't you? I'll pack now—I'm so sorry, Aunty, to mess you about like this——'

'Get away with you. You couldn't stay here with that going on. I'll come and help you in a minute.'

Fate was on her side. She caught a train with five minutes to spare, and sat down, too agitated to read the newspaper her aunt had thrust into her hand at the station. She stared out of the window with unseeing eyes, and scarcely noticed when the rain started.

There was a half hour wait at one station to pick up the connection to Rathiemore, and by now the rain was a torrent. The ferry ride across to the island, although a mere three miles, was a choppy crossing, and Jan, after seven hours' travelling, was hungry and cold and in a bad temper. There would be no one to meet her, and it was a three-mile walk to Craigie House, and she would be soaked by the time she reached it, but she no longer cared.

Early evening, and dark beause of the rain and low heavy clouds, and it matched her mood perfectly as she set off to trudge along the road, keeping dead centre to avoid the treacherous ditches at either side that would now be like quagmires. Bleak hills towered darkly on both sides. They had given the island its name hundreds of years ago, and Craigie House had been built over a century previously and as far as Jan was concerned, was as much a part of the island as the hills themselves. Set in a deeply wooded area near to the water, a crumbling granite building covered with ivy, it was the only home Jan had ever known, and no stranger was going to come and try and take—she rounded a curve in the shadowy road, and because of the driving rain, and because her head was lowered, she neither heard nor saw the rapidly approaching vehicle until the blazing headlights and screech of tortured brakes jerked her head up in sudden shock. Trembling, she stood quite still, bathed in the light from the Land-Rover which had stopped less than three feet away from her, not straight, but slewed across the road at an odd angle.

She took a deep shaky breath, and a giant of a man jumped down from the driver's seat, and strode across to her and said, in the most *furious* voice she had ever heard in her life:

'What the *hell* do you think you're doing walking in the middle of the road like that, you *stupid* idiot!'

Jan had had a day that had begun badly, and got progressively worse, and not only was she cold, hungry, tired, and wet, but she had just nearly been run over by this brute of a man she couldn't even see. And he had the nerve to speak to her as though it was *her* fault! Her hair was black, but the way her temper was, it should have been fiery red. Her case thudded to the ground.

'Listen, *you!*' she began. 'You came thundering round the corner at about seventy——'

'Twenty,' he interrupted, but she ignored it

9

completely.

'Miles an hour, nearly run me over—and then have the utter gall to tell me off! You're a road hog of the worst kind, a typical *man* driver, completely arrogant and selfish. Don't you dare speak to me like that! I've a good mind to report you to the police!' She was shaking with rage—and then he began to *laugh*. Mockingly, which was worse.

'Report *me*? What for? My God, you've got a cheek! You've no right to be walking dead centre in the dark. Look at you,' a hand came out and contemptuously pointed at her. 'You're not even wearing a single item of light clothing. Let me tell you something. You're lucky I saw you.'

The temper was draining away from Jan. Because in spite of both their angers, there was a hard core of truth in his last words. She could easily have been knocked over—and her journey home would not have done anyone any good. Yet there was his arrogance. It would not allow her to apologize to a man so completely and utterly aggressive.

She picked up her case. Better not let him see the trembling either. Just to leave with dignity would be enough.

'Then I must thank you for *not* running me over,' she said, surprised at how calmly she was managing to speak. 'If you'll let me pass, you can be on your way.' But strangely enough, he didn't move, just remained standing in front of her, blocking her way. And he really was big. Over six foot and broad-shouldered with it.

'You're shaking like a leaf,' he said. 'Scared?'

'I'm not shaking or scared,' she answered sharply. 'I'm tired, that's all. And this case is heavy. If you *don't* mind?' pointedly.

He lifted the case out of her hand so quickly that it didn't give her time to resist.

'Hmm, reasonably heavy—for a slip of a girl like you,' he answered, and there was that touch of mockery again which set the hairs prickling on the back of her neck. 'So the least I can do is take it—and you—to your destination. Where to?'

'Thank you, I don't——'

'Oh, come off it,' he said. 'I'm not standing here getting soaked making impolite small talk with *you* all night. Just state your destination and I'll see you get there without being run over by any more male chauvinist pigs.'

She took a deep breath. And counted five this time. Before she felt the urge to hit him hard. 'I'm going to Craigie House,' she answered—and before she had finished the last word he began to laugh.

'I don't believe it!' he said, when he could speak. '*You're* the other sister! *Now* I see what they meant! I should have known!'

Something—something utterly *awful* began to penetrate Jan's tired brain. The hairs on her neck prickled again, and a cold sensation crept down her spine as she looked up into the shadowy face she had not yet seen properly.

'*You* are the man——' she began, and stopped.

'Yes? The man who?' he enquired delicately.

'Give me my case. I'm not going anywhere with you.' She tried to snatch it from him, but it was about as effective a move as a child's would have been.

He turned abruptly and strode to the vehicle, and she, having no choice, followed him. He flung her case in the back, and held the passenger door open.

'Get in,' he said. 'Unless you want me to throw you in like that case.'

She climbed in. For at that moment she wasn't sure if he'd do it, and she didn't want to find out. He was adequately capable of doing so, she knew that.

He reversed the Land-Rover and they drove along towards Craigie House. Her home. One thing was sure—the telegram had not come a moment too soon. Nor had it exaggerated. If this man was staying at her home, then her father must be mad.

He scrunched to a stop by the front door and leaned over to pick up her case from behind her. 'Out you get,' he said. 'We're here.'

She turned and looked at him. 'I don't know what your name is,' she said, speaking calmly and slowly, just to make sure he heard every word. 'But I need no one to tell me when I reach *my* home. Thank you.'

'The name's Breck Fallon,' he answered. 'And yours is Janis, only everyone calls you Jan.'

'My word!' she said. 'You've been doing your homework, haven't you?'

'Not really. You seem to be the general topic of conversation round this place. It's Jan this and Jan that, and "I wonder what Jan would say?" and so naturally I was curious to meet this formidable personage whose opinions seemed to be so terribly important. And now I have,' and he paused. He switched the light on in the vehicle, and she was able to see his face clearly for the first time. And something stirred within her, a prickle of fear. Thick black brows over sooty-lashed eyes were the predominant feature. She couldn't see the precise colour of his eyes—but that seemed unimportant—a strongly shaped face with high cheekbones, a beautifully shaped mouth—only the amused quirk seemed slightly to spoil it to Jan's eyes, and she snapped, before she could help herself:

'And?'

'And what do I find? Why'—and he lifted one finger and put it under her chin, and tilted it upwards—'she's just a little girl after all, and a hot-tempered one at that. Nothing to worry about *at* all.' And he grinned, a flash of white teeth showing in the dusky light. Jan lifted her hand and pushed his away.

'Keep your hands well away from me, *Mister* Breck Fallon,' she said, holding tight to the temper she felt rising within her, 'or you might find I've got claws as well.'

He sucked in his breath in a dark 'ah'. He had a deep voice too, she noticed inconsequently. 'Threats? See how I tremble!' She had had enough. She turned away from him and lifted the door catch to open it—only it was jammed.

He leaned over, taking his time. 'Dear me,' he said. 'It does seem to be stuck, doesn't it? That's the trouble with these new-fangled machines——'

It wasn't her imagination, he was mocking her in a way that was vaguely uncomfortable. Almost as if he *knew* something. 'There. Done it.' The door swung open, she was released from the intolerable prison of his nearness, and she jumped down to the ground and stalked away to the house. Her first task—her very first—was a word with her father.

'Hoy!' That deep, insolent voice arrested her. She turned, very slowly.

'Your case. Remember?' Then as she began to

walk back to the Land-Rover, he added: 'I'll get it. Just thought I'd tell you in case there was anything you needed urgently. Off you go, little girl. I'll follow.'

'Don't call me little girl again,' she said—slowly.

'You don't like it? Sorry, honey, I'll try to remember. Trouble is,' he added in a confidential tone, 'I've got a bad memory.'

They were in the porch, he pushed the door open, and the light flooded out, and she saw him again even more clearly.

There was no mistaking the powerful build of him, the width of the shoulders, the easy athletic way he loped in beside her, the arrogant 'at home' manner of him. And Jan experienced a stab of apprehension. This was no ordinary man. There was something special about him. She didn't yet know what it was. He put down her case and looked at her.

'No welcoming committee?' he said quietly. 'Shame. Didn't they know you were coming?'

'No,' she said shortly. 'Thanks for the lift. Don't let me detain you. You *were* on your way somewhere?'

'Oh yes, only to the village to phone. It can wait. The pleasure of bringing you home has more than compensated——'

'Please don't waste your time on stupid remarks,' she said. 'I'm too tired to appreciate them.' She looked at her suitcase. 'I'm away to have a word with my father. Unless you have any objection?' she added, very sweetly.

'Me? Hardly. I'll say goodnight, then, Jan—if I may call you that.'

'You may call me what you like—it won't be for

long,' and with that parting shot she walked along the wide hall and into the sitting room, where she knew she would find her father.

She heard the front door close quietly as she entered the room. And she smiled to herself. She wondered what he would make of that remark.

'Jan! What on earth——?' There was no mistaking the look on her father's face as he rose from his seat by the fire and came forward to greet her. It was the look worn by a schoolboy who has been caught smoking behind the garden shed. Jan hugged him.

'Hello, Dad—yes, I thought I'd get home again —I've had enough of the bright lights of Edinburgh.' And she winked at her two sisters, whose faces shone with innocent surprise. 'Hello, Judy, Helen,' she greeted them.

'Er—Ina's not ill, is she?' her father enquired anxiously. 'I mean, with you——'

'Aunt Ina? No, she's fine. As I say, I just decided I wanted to be home.' And now was the time, before he had got over the shock of her arrival. 'I was nearly run over by a very odd man on my way here.' She fixed him firmly with her dark eyes. 'Says his name's Breck Fallon—huh!' She was well aware that her two younger sisters were trying to stifle giggles as they hid behind their books, but she was busy watching Cedric Sutherland as he tried to nonchalantly fill his pipe. He doesn't really belong to the twentieth century, she thought, as she looked at the aquiline profile so intent on his task. He should be living in the seventeenth century, at a gentler pace, pottering about his garden, inventing his inventions, studying the stars... A rush of anger against the dark intruder filled her. But she wasn't going to be too soft on him even so. Because he was unworldly, he needed protection ...

'Ah, Fallon! Yes.' She sat down on the ancient settee beside him, and a spring twanged protestingly. It really ought to be replaced ... 'You've—er—met him, then?' And their eyes met.

Jan smiled gently. 'Yes, Dad, we have—to put it mildly. He's staying here, is he?'

'Oh, ah, yes, for a few days, a few days,' he nodded wisely and puffed hard on his pipe, and Jan thought: A lot of 'ah's' and 'oh's' is a sure sign he's uncomfortable.

'Where's he from?'

'Ah—er—London, I believe. He's—er—the son of an old friend of mine.'

'Really? Anyone we know?' Judy and Helen had given up all pretence of reading now. They were listening, frankly agog. Judy at seventeen, leggy and thin and a confirmed man-hater, Helen at fifteen softer and gentler, like her father, both with Jan's dark eyes and hair.

'Ah—no, I think not, my dear.' The pipe appeared to have gone out. There was a great play of relighting it and her father's voice seemed slightly muffled as he went on: 'In the war, you know—mmm—knew many men—mmm—very old chum.'

'Hmm, I see,' Jan nodded. It was worse than she had imagined. He was lying—and not very well either, because he wasn't used to it, so it must be serious. She had done all she could for the moment. The very next task was a word with her two sisters.

'I'm starving,' she said, as she stood up, 'and soaking. I'll go and change, and then get myself something to eat.'

'We had stew,' said Helen, 'there's some left. I'll

go and warm it.'

'I'll come with you,' announced Judy. 'So we'll see you in the kitchen. Don't be long.'

'I shan't be.' Jan gave her father a sweet smile. 'I'll be down in five minutes.' She sailed out of the room.

'Now,' said Jan, as she sat curled up on a kitchen chair wrapped in her old blue dressing gown. 'Tell me ALL.'

'There's a lot to tell,' Judy warned. 'You'd better eat up first. We don't want you choking over the lovely stew that Helen made——'

'Well, at least I *try*—which is more than I can say of some——'

'Quiet!' Jan shouted. '*Please*. no arguing. We're all in this together, so we'll have no petty squabbling over food—hey, there's a thought. Did *he* eat it?'

'Well—yes,' Judy admitted, after a moment's thought. 'But have you seen the size of him? I mean, he'd have to keep stoked up or he'd fade away and die, wouldn't he?'

'Mm, that's what I mean,' nodded Jan, with a light in her eyes. 'I wonder if he enjoys cold lumpy porridge for breakfast?'

'You wouldn't *dare*,' breathed Helen.

'Oh, wouldn't I?'

'Daddy was telling him what a marvellous cook you were anyway,' said Judy helpfully. 'Practically up to Cordon Bleu standard.'

'Well, he'll be in for even more of a shock, won't he?' and Jan began to laugh quietly. Then, sobering, as she remembered what they were really there for, she said: 'Right, let's get sorted out. First—

why is he here?'

'Daddy says he's the son of an old friend,' Helen answered.

'Yes, he told me that too—and very uncomfortable he looked when he said it. No, what happened when he first arrived? Tell me everyting.'

The two younger girls looked at one another, pondering. Then Judy, as the elder, spoke. 'Right,' she said. 'You went off to Edinburgh on Monday. Helen and I played tennis, and Daddy vanished into the den to work on one of his inventions—he said—and everything was quite normal. Then in the evening he made a phone call—again from the extension in his den, and we thought it was a bit odd because he never said who it was to, you know, like he usually does.' Jan nodded impatiently.

'Yes, go on.'

'That was all. Then, on Tuesday morning——' she paused dramatically, 'Helen and I were giving the old playroom a good clear out for a jumble sale in Rathiemore and we heard this car stopping at the front door. We dived to the window because it wasn't the day for the butcher, and——' She widened her eyes dramatically, and Helen burst out:

'*He* got out of this Land-Rover, and just stood there looking at the house.'

'Yes, *and* he looked up and saw us!' Judy added. 'Cheeky devil!'

'Go on,' Jan said urgently, and the other two looked at one another, and Judy went on:

'Well, it was odd then, because we'd sort of dodged back, but we heard Daddy's voice from the front door, so we crept to the window again to peep, and Daddy was shaking hands and saying things like: "What a pleasant surprise" and "How nice to see you"—but it was all very loud, almost as though——' she paused, and Jan said softly:

'Almost as though he was saying it for your benefit?'

'Yes! That's it!' Both girls nodded. 'Wasn't that strange?'

'Yes, it was. What then?'

'Well, then we heard them coming in, so we went to the top of the stairs to try and listen, but they'd gone in the den, and we couldn't hear a *thing.*'

The picture was very clear in Jan's mind, and the more she heard, the more uneasy she grew.

'So we went down after a while, *very* casually, and Daddy introduced us to him—and *I* didn't like him at all,' said Judy, then added, giving her younger sister a withering look: '*She* said she thought he was rather dishy.'

'I didn't!' Helen exclaimed, going a warm shade of pink. 'I merely remarked that he wasn't—he wasn't—well, bad looking.'

Judy snorted. 'Huh! You went all soppy.'

'Cut it out!' Jan intervened. 'Never mind *that.* What's all this about him looking around the house? That's the bit I want to hear.'

'Well, Daddy was all jolly at lunch, and saying that he must show him round, and Breck was saying what a good idea, and how lucky he'd chanced to hear that Daddy lived here and everything——'

'You mean he just happened to be passing?'

'That's the impression he and Daddy seemed to be trying to give, but it didn't fool *us*, I can tell you, so after a lot of thought we decided to send you that telegram.'

'And I'm very glad that you did,' said Jan firmly.

'Both of you. You've done the right thing.'

'Oh, I'm so glad you're back,' Helen sighed. 'We felt so helpless. You'll look after everything, won't you? You won't let Daddy sell the house?'

'Not in a thousand years.'

'You don't think he's a thief, do you?' Judy said. She looked as though she had been giving deep thought to something for quite a few minutes. 'I mean, he couldn't be here to steal any of Daddy's inventions?'

'Well, if he was,' reasoned Jan, 'surely Daddy wouldn't welcome him like an old friend?'

'Well, no, but suppose he's *pretending* to want to buy the house, and lulling his suspicions that way, and really is after *something else*?' She made it sound incredibly sinister.

Jan frowned. 'We mustn't discard any possibility —ah! there's something *I've* just remembered. When we had our near-collision he said he was on his way to phone. But why not use this one?'

'Obvious,' answered Judy, who read more than her share of thrillers. 'He's in the pay of a foreign power, and has to make special coded messages.'

'Or quite simply didn't want anyone here to know where he was phoning,' Jan went on. 'Mmm, I don't like this Breck Fallon at all—and that name of his is a phoney if ever I've heard one——' and as she said the words, the subject of them walked into the kitchen, and said:

'I assure you it's not.'

CHAPTER TWO

THREE startled pairs of eyes looked up into a pair of steady grey ones. Very cool grey ones. Breck Fallon smiled, very slowly, and added:

'I'm sorry to disappoint you ladies, but that is the name on my driving licence—and a few other things.'

Jan looked at him coolly, composure regained. 'We were having a private conversation,' she said. 'Did you want something?'

'Yes, I did,' he answered. 'And I don't listen to private conversations, I do assure you, but I could hardly avoid hearing my name. You did say it quite distinctly.' The cool grey had turned to steel now. It was as though there were only the two of them in the room, the way his eyes met and challenged hers. He stood there by the door and in a strange way it was as though she was seeing him for the first time, now, properly, with the light upon him, casting shadows on the lower part of his face, emphasising the hardness of his eyes—mocking eyes—arrogant eyes, drawing all the strength from her, making her go weak, threatening her. His hair was black, but flecked with grey, and he was tanned and healthy-looking, and that square chin had a determination about it that made Jan want to turn and run. And if she did, the battle would be lost before it was begun.

She swallowed hard, and stood up, forgetting that she wore her ancient dressing gown over her nightie, and said the first words that came into her confused brain: 'What do you want?'

'Why, a cup of tea,' he said, and his tone was quite gentle because he knew what effect he'd had, and perhaps it had satisfied him. 'Your father and I were talking, and he said he'd like one, so I offered to come out and do so—I'm sorry, I didn't realize you were ready for bed.' But he smiled as he said those last few words, and cast a slow glance up and down the length of the garment. Jan sat down again. Not too quickly, but fast enough, biting back her mortification.

Helen jumped up. 'I'll put the kettle on for you Mr.—er—Breck,' she looked slightly shamefacedly at Jan as she went to the sink.

'Thanks, Helen, that's kind of you,' he sat on a corner of the scrubbed wooden table, and then he looked across at Jan. 'Feeling better after the unfortunate incident?' he enquired casually.

'Yes, thank you.' Oh, how she wished she had put on her other dressing gown, the red velvet one she kept for holidays. Not that it was important, but ... It would have been better for her morale.

'Good.' He nodded in a kindly fashion.

'Did you make your phone call?' she asked, remembering, thinking: that'll have him.

'Oh! Yes, thanks.'

'You could have phoned from here. My father wouldn't have minded, I'm sure,' she said, feeling better every minute. From behind her the kettle began its long sad whistle and she heard the clatter of the teapot as Helen put it on the stove. Everything, every sound, every shadow, was clearly defined in that room, because Jan was sharply aware of it all. Because he was there. He was having an odd effect on her, but she didn't know what it was.

'Of course, I dare say I could. But I had to go down to the inn for cigarettes and a bottle of whisky, so it seemed logical to me to make my call from there.' He gave her a slow, charming smile, and added: 'Your father and I are going to have a drop after the tea. You'll join us, of course—I mean, you're not too *young* to drink, are you?' This with such an air of bland innocence that for a moment the insult didn't register. Then it did.

'I'm twenty-one,' she answered slowly. Oh, heavens, don't let me hit him now, she prayed, not in front of these two, but I've never met a man I've so disliked——

'Really?' His teeth were good and strong, and all his own from the looks of it. 'I'm so sorry. I thought——' he shrugged. 'Well, never mind. Ah, tea ready. Thanks, Helen, you're very kind.' He picked up two beakers in one hand, teapot in the other, turned and nodded at Jan, and then walked out.

Judy shut the door after him, and leaned against it. 'Wow!' she said.

'I could have hit him!' exploded Jan. 'I *hate* him!'

'I know. It shows,' Judy grimaced. 'And I don't think he's terribly fond of you either. Cor! I wouldn't like to be in a fight with *him*.'

'Well, we are, metaphorically speaking,' Jan said grimly. 'And it's three against one, let's remember *that*. I'll not be beaten by any toffee-nosed Londoner who tries to imply we're a simple lot of peasants. The *nerve*——' she stood and went to the stove. 'I need a drink. Coffee, anyone?'

As they sat brooding over their beakers of hot

coffee, Jan looked round her. Craigie House was old, and needed many things doing—jobs that just could not be afforded, because there was no money to do them. She and her sisters worked hard, and had learned to turn their hands to most tasks in that vast mansion, decorating, painting, minor plastering—but they all knew that it wasn't enough. Many thousands would have to be spent on it to make it immaculate. Was Breck Fallon the man with money to do so?

'It's like the Forth Bridge,' she said suddenly.

Judy and Helen looked at her. 'What?' they said in chorus.

'You know. They never finish painting that, do they? No sooner have they finished than it's time to start again—this house is like that. Whatever we do, there's always more—and more. We must make him *see* that. Then he won't be so keen.'

'You mean keep pointing out all its faults?' Judy suggested.

'Right.'

'But—but isn't it a bit disloyal?' Helen spoke gently. 'I mean, it's our house, and we love it, and I'd feel awful if I was going round poking holes in it, metaphorically speaking. I'd feel as if I were hurting its feelings.'

'All's fair in love and war,' said Jan, squashing her own momentary doubts on that subject. 'It's all for our own good, isn't it? And when we've got rid of *him*, we'll do all the jobs that need doing, so that will be all right.' She sipped her coffee. 'I mean, we don't want *him* living here, do we?'

'If that's what we're sure he's after,' said Judy.

'What else?'

'I don't know,' Judy shrugged helplessly. 'We've

24

both gone over it in our minds, and there's nothing else. Unless we're imagining it all, and he really is the son of an old friend of Daddy's who just happened to be passing——'

'Hah! We all know when Daddy's not telling the truth, don't we? And anyway, how can anyone be "just passing" this place? We're not on the main route from Edinburgh to Inverness or anything. We're living on a remote island that has to be visited by ferry—and no one comes here at all, not even tourists.'

'So why,' said Helen, the thinker, 'should he want to come and live here? We've seen him—he looks like someone who enjoys the bright lights, and night clubs and things—he doesn't look like a man who'd be happy sitting fishing for hours—and let's face it, there's not much else to do here—unless he likes knitting.'

'Hmm, good point.' Jan chewed her lip. 'This mystery deepens by the minute. What room is he sleeping in?'

Her sisters looked at her blankly, then Helen said: 'The blue one at the back. Why?'

A slow smile lit Jan's face. 'I think I'd like to have a little look round——' she was stopped by the gasp of horror from the other two.

'Relax,' she said mildly. 'Only a quick peep, that's all. After all, I shall need to go in and make our guest's bed in the morning, won't I? And if it happens that I go up when he's busy eating breakfast—well——' she shrugged slowly.

'He made his own bed this morning,' said Helen. 'Because I went in to do it and it was all tidy.'

'Hmm, well, never mind, I'm not to know *that*, am I? I'll take a duster as well, and the polish.

What sort of luggage has he got?'

'Three super suitcases plastered with labels from all over the place, and a super-looking camera that he left on the dressing table, *and* he uses some terribly expensive after-shave lotion that smells like mountains and forests, *and* one of those battery razors that's got a very foreign name on it, and looks very swish.'

'My God!' Jan stared at her in open admiration. 'You don't do so badly yourself, love. What sort of labels—I mean where from? Did you read any?'

'Oh yes,' Helen nodded innocently, and began to reel off names as if she had rehearsed it. 'Monte Carlo—Rio de Janeiro—Mockba—that's Moscow, isn't it?—Sydney—New York—those were the clearer ones, the others were more faded, but I think there was one from the Q.E. 2 as well, I *think*.'

There was a pause while they digested this richness of information.

'I don't suppose,' said Judy wistfully, 'that he could be a *spy* or anything?'

'No,' answered Jan. 'But I'm liking him less and less every minute. I think we must try and keep a watch on Daddy—I mean, try and avoid letting them be alone together for too long. You know how unworldly he is. A man like that could impress him no end, and talk him into anything. Agreed?'

'Agreed,' they nodded.

'Right.' Jan stood up. 'Let's join them—*now*. Let's hope we're not too late.'

'Are you going like *that*?' Judy enquired.

Jan looked down at her dressing gown. Not for the world would she admit that she would have given anything to be in the red velvet. 'Certainly,' she answered firmly. 'It's *quite* respectable, and I'm certainly not out to impress *him*. Come on, girls. Let battle commence!'

The trouble was, Jan had to admit to herself the following morning when she woke up, that Breck Fallon seemed a very wary customer, not at all the normal kind of man. He had greeted them with apparent delight when they had trooped into the sitting room, stood up most politely to give Jan his chair, and then launched into an immediate discussion on tennis. Did they play? he wondered. He had seen the tennis court at the back of the house from his bedroom window, and thought how *nice* it must be to have your very own court. Of course, he had shrugged, he rarely played—and Jan had said, before her sisters could: 'Then perhaps you'd like a game tomorrow?' and she had smiled, and hoped he wouldn't see the expression on the girls' faces as she added: 'Of course, I'm not very good—but I'm sure it would help to pass half an hour or so, there's so little to do here.'

'Fine.' He looked pleased. 'You won't mind if we have a practice first? I've not played for years.'

'Of course not.' She had smiled pleasantly, and raised her whisky glass.

'Cheers.'

She sat up in bed, remembering those events now as the door opened and Helen rushed in and settled on the foot of the bed. 'You're really playing?' Helen asked.

'Of course.' Jan smiled. 'Just keep your fingers crossed for me.'

'I nearly laughed out loud when you said you weren't any good, Jan. How *could* you? I hope he's hasn't seen your cups.'

'I hid them before I went to bed,' Jan answered calmly. 'I'd just like to dent the man's ego a bit, that's all. If he rides around all the time I bet he doesn't get enough exercise.'

'But he'll be a lot stronger in any case—he's bound to be. Men are.'

'I know. But it's skill that can count—and speed. I've got both.' Jan grinned impishly. 'All right, I know I sound bigheaded, but I'd like to see his face when he's beaten. I bet he's a rotten loser.'

'Isn't it a bit unsporting not to tell him you've played in schools internationals——' began Helen dubiously.

'No! Besides, as you pointed out, he's a lot stronger. I may lose,' Jan finished consolingly, but she had no intention of doing so, none at all.

She served him his porridge in the dining room, relieved that her father had not yet come down as she apologized blandly for it being cool. 'It's so *far* from the kitchen to here,' she said sweetly. 'This house is so *old*, you see, and well, you know how long it takes to get from the kitchen.' And she sighed eloquently. She didn't add that she had left the plate on the kitchen table for several minutes before bringing it in.

'Quite all right,' he answered. 'It's delicious, I assure you.'

'My sister is making the bacon and egg,' she went on, sipping her orange juice.

'I hope you have a good appetite.'

'Oh yes, and besides, I need to keep my strength up for this game of tennis.' He smiled gently. It was a slightly crooked smile, not unattractive, she was forced—reluctantly—to admit. 'I'm looking forward to it. It's very kind of you to spare the time.'

'Not at all,' she poured a cup of coffee for him and he thanked her. 'There's not much else to do—except housework, of course—a place this size needs a lot of looking after, as you can imagine,' and she sighed very softly.

'Would you prefer to live in something smaller?' he asked.

Alarm flared in her eyes. 'No!' the word came out too sharply. 'No,' she repeated, more casually. 'This is my home. I wouldn't change it, but I don't blind myself to its faults.'

'Very practical.' Helen came in with a plate of bacon and egg, and Jan averted her eyes from it and began to butter a piece of cold toast.

'You're eating very little,' Breck remarked.

'I rarely eat breakfast,' she answered. 'I'm only here to keep you company.

'Ah, the perfect hostess,' he murmured, and for some reason she found herself going warm. Oh, I'm looking forward to beating you into the ground, she thought. It will be a pleasure.

She bit into the toast and watched him eating his breakfast. The sun shone in behind him, casting a golden haze round his outline as he sat at the table. He wore a white tee-shirt with denim jacket over it, and matching denim jeans. The clothes were well worn but had an expensive air about them, a casual look that suited him. *He* looked casual—as if he didn't give a damn about anything, and his lean strong features were not filled with aggression, but almost calm. Yet it was deceptive, she felt sure. This was no quiet man, there was an explosive quality to him. She had glimpsed it briefly the pre-

vious night at their first unfortunate encounter—
then afterwards, in the kitchen, when he had over-
heard her comments about his name—the suppressed explosiveness of a volcano capable of erup-
tion. But clever with it, for his behaviour since had
been beyond criticism—and yet ... there was *something* there all the time, something that Jan didn't
understand, a subtle awareness that she could only
glimpse, yet not fully comprehend. Instinct told her
to be on her guard. Even his most innocent remarks had a quality about them ...

'You're very quiet,' he said almost mildly, nothing wrong with that. But ...

'Am I? I'm sorry, I was just thinking.' And I'm
not going to tell you what about, she thought.

'Don't apologize. We all need time to think. And
you don't have the distractions of radio and television here, I notice——'

'Those!' Her eyes sparkled. 'There's a radio in
the kitchen. We get the news on it every day, and
that's about all. As for television——' and she
stopped, because in a minute she would give herself away.

'Ah! A sore point. You can't receive TV here, I
take it?'

She looked blankly at him. Did he actually
think——? 'Receive it? Of course we can—if we
wanted. But we don't. It's the most stupid thing
that's ever been invented—the most useless, soul-
destroying device——' she paused for breath.

'You *all* think that? Or is this just your opinion?'

'Of course we all do!' She glared at him, forgetting all her intentions of not being drawn into anything at all personal. 'There are far too many

things to do without sitting glued for hours to a box of moving wallpaper——'

He stifled what could have been a laugh, and Jan half rose, ready to walk out, and he said quickly: 'I'm sorry, but you have such a vivid way of expressing yourself. Tell me, am I mistaken, or did your father tell me you had a sister in London who's married to someone in television?'

She sat down again. Slowly. 'Oh,' she said. 'I *see*. You knew all along. Was this your idea of a joke?'

'No.' He looked quite serious. 'I wanted to hear your opinions on the subject, that's all. You see, I wouldn't believe what your father told me, that your way of life is so important to you, just as it is, that any change in it would only be for the worse——'

'You've been talking about me?' she asked dully. 'My father has been talking about this—to you?'

'I'm sorry. It was my fault. I merely expressed surprise at not seeing a TV set in the corner, and he mentioned that it wasn't—er—popular here.'

Jan stood up. 'If you'll excuse me,' she said, 'I'll clear these plates away.' She didn't want to stay talking to him any longer. He had a most disconcerting effect on her, and she didn't feel able to cope any longer.

'Certainly. I'll not be a moment. What time do you want to play tennis?'

She looked at him. 'When you're ready. Any time.'

'Say half an hour? I have one or two letters to write, and then——' he shrugged. 'Then I'm all yours.'

'Half an hour it is.' She walked out of the room quickly. 'Then I'm all yours,' he had said. What an

31

odd thing to say! And what a strange man altogether. The kind of man it would be difficult—nay, impossible, to ignore, under any circumstances, for he exuded an air of power, of dominance, although it was well concealed most of the time. Yet Jan could feel it. It was there—and in a way, she was almost frightened of him. It was ridiculous of course—quite *absurd* to feel so, but she was almost regretting her foolish challenge to a tennis match.

The small wistful hope that it might rain was banished the instant they set foot out of the kitchen door. The sun blazed down from an almost white sky, and everything was so green and lovely that Jan blinked. It was weather like this that could persuade even the hardened city-dweller to move to an island...

'Beautiful day.' The man beside her might have read her thoughts.

'Yes,' she answered. 'We have an awful lot of rain—as you will have gathered from last night.'

'Oh yes, I already know that. Your sisters told me,' he added dryly. 'But the main thing is that it's not raining now. What surface is there on the court?'

'Oh! Shale.'

'Hmm, I see.' She looked at him, wondering at the question. The tennis court was at the end of the kitchen garden, which was bursting with growing vegetables of all kinds, ably looked after by Jan and her sisters.

He commented on the profusion as they passed, and she answered: 'Oh, they're essential. Fresh produce only comes over once a week from the mainland, and tinned foods are too expensive, so,' she shrugged gracefully, 'we grow our own.' Then she added quickly: 'Do you like gardening?'

Breck laughed. 'I was waiting for you to ask that. No—but I dare say I'd learn, if I had to.' Quietly spoken, the last four words held—to Jan's ears—a tone of menace. She bit her lip in irritation. It was quite stupid of her to let everything he said assume a great significance. But that was the way it was— that was the way he affected her. She looked forward to the tennis court in front of them, and then down to the racquet she held. She had embarked upon a deliberate pretence. She had more or less told him that she was an indifferent player when in fact she was extremely good, and practised as often as time allowed. And she had done it simply because he had managed to get under her skin in so many ways from the moment of their first unfortunate meeting on the road home. I'm being childish, she thought suddenly. Utterly childish—and yet it was too late to do anything about it now. She was committed. She suddenly wanted to admit her deception—yet she could not. She did not know how. She was to wish afterwards, when it was too late, that she had done so.

'Right. Which end?' she asked.

'Either.'

'You're the guest,' she insisted, and was aware of the slightly amused look he gave her. 'Take the far end to begin with, the sun is behind you there.'

'Fair enough.' He paused by the net. 'Is this okay?'

'Yes.' She sent a ball across to him, and they began the practice. She wondered if Judy and Helen were watching from a window—and where their father was. He sent the balls back well enough, hesitantly at first, then as they warmed up, more skilfully. But there was no power in the strokes; it seemed as if he was content merely to return, to keep the ball moving, and when Jan called: 'Shall we begin?' he nodded.

'Best of three sets?' he asked.

'Yes.' The tingle was in her blood. Her reasons for coming out were forgotten—as were her doubts. She was going to play the game she loved best, and she was going to beat him. He served first, and she waited for the ball, and it could have been a stranger she was playing now.

When the score in that first game was thirty-forty, she sent a long low powerful reply to his serve that was quite unreturnable.

'Shot!' he called, and she could have sworn there was admiration in his voice. 'First game to you.'

Her serve was as powerful as the average man's. Sizzling across the court, her first one had him looking to see where it had gone, then he grinned at her.

'Fifteen-love,' he called. 'Was that a fluke?'

'I don't know,' she answered, and then sent him another one, equally swift—only this time he returned it—and then suddenly his play was no longer hesitant, and he was moving faster than he had at first. Not only that, but he was sending the balls spinning back at her in a way she had not encountered before, making her run, keeping her on her toes, so that to serve her best was not enough, she had to be constantly on her guard because his returns were devastating.

He won the second game, and the third. And in the fourth, when it was her turn to serve again, and he was leading by three games to one, Jan began to realize something she should have done before. She was not playing tennis with a beginner or anything remotely like it. She was up against a far worthier—and more powerful—opponent than any she had encountered in her life. It stimulated her. She put all she had into that fourth game because it was vital for her to win it. She sent across her most skilful, forceful serves, never relaxed for an instant, and when the score was deuce she slammed a fluke shot that had him spinning round in laughing surprise.

'Vantage server,' he called. This was it. She *had* to win this point. Jan stood for a moment before beginning the swing up to her serve. 'Let it be a scorcher,' she muttered almost silently. It was. And the game was hers. But her victory was a temporary one. He won the next three games quite effortlessly.

Jan thought that she would be glad of the brief respite when the set finished, and went to the bench at the side of the court trying to control the slight tremor in her legs. She looked up at the sky, because it seemed to her that the sun must be blazing down, so hot was she, but it had vanished behind a cloud. Her eyes met those of Breck, and in his was something intensely disturbing. She found out what it was the next moment when he said softly:

'Well, well, I must say I enjoyed that set. I hope you did?'

She had to swallow before she could speak. 'Yes. I thought you'd not played for years?'

'Did I say that?' He was so big, somehow intimidating, and she regretted her question, but it was too late. It had been said, and now he was about to answer her, and instinct told her that she would not like what he was going to say. 'It was a little white lie—on the lines of yours.'

'What—what do you mean?' But she already knew. He took off his denim jacket and slung it over the back of the old wooden bench.

'You told me you weren't very good. And you could hardly hide your delight when I told you I'd not played for ages. You *know* you're damn good—and you thought you'd teach me a little lesson, didn't you?' There was nothing on his face save a cool expression of polite indifference, but his words belied his look. They were hard—as hard as him. Jan half turned away and he reached out to touch her arm.

'Don't look away when I'm speaking to you. It's about time someone told you a few home truths—and that's what I'm going to do.'

She swung back angrily. 'Who are *you* to speak to *me* like that? I don't have to stand here listening to you being rude, I assure you, *Mister* Breck Fallon.'

'Well, you're going to. Whether you like it or not. You made a slight mistake when you hid your cups for tennis—you were a few hours too late. I'd already seen them.'

It was at that moment that Jan wished she had revealed her deception before the game started. But not for anything would she have admitted it. She lifted her chin.

'All right, so you knew. That makes us quits, doesn't it?'

'Not quite.' He paused. 'There are several other things that need to be brought out in the open. Now is as good a time as any. After all, you've got nowhere to dash off to, have you? As you are always

36

reminding me, for reasons best known to yourself, there's *so* little to do here.'

She didn't like his tone, his stance, his looks, or anything about him, for that matter. But there was nothing she could do about it, and no way to fight him. He was completely in charge.

He pointed to the bench. 'Why don't you sit down? You look hot and tired.'

'I can stand, thank you,' she answered. 'But don't let me stop *you* sitting down if you feel the need.'

The corner of his wide mouth twitched, but only for an instant. 'Quick-tongued and quick-tempered,' he said. 'I'd know you anywhere.' She didn't understand his last words—but she soon would. 'So let's have it, little Miss Spitfire. Get it off your chest. *Why* are you so obviously trying to get rid of me?'

The bluntness of his words was an almost physical shock. But he had asked, and so she would tell him.

'Because I love my home, and so do my sisters. And so does my father, whether you believe that or not—and he can't help being a dreamer, and impractical—and he's too easy to take advantage of, but we don't want him to sell our house and we'll fight it, and we'll fight *you*——' her eyes sparkled, her cheeks were pink, and she didn't realize how beautiful and defiant she looked. So intent was she on what she needed to say that nothing mattered except making him understand.

'But I don't want to buy your house. Is that what you thought?' He sounded almost amused. 'Is that *really* what you thought?' In a minute he would be laughing. Jan stared at him. She was unable to speak for a moment. A huge relief flooded her.

37

'You don't—you're not——' she began, and stopped. Because there was something else on his face now. A deep, knowing look. An expression almost of concern. The relief ebbed away.

'I think you'd better sit down,' he said. 'Because I do have something to tell you—and I don't think you're going to like it.'

CHAPTER THREE

JAN moved to the bench. The relief had gone, replaced by a peculiar kind of numbness. Breck Fallon stood beside her, and put one foot up on the hard wooden seat. He looked completely relaxed, and yet she sensed a kind of tautness about him that communicated itself to her.

'I don't understand,' she said faintly. 'If you don't want to buy our house—what is it?'

There was silence for a few moments, and everything was so intensified for Jan that she could hear a bee busily rooting in a flower a few yards away. She was also conscious of her heartbeats. Distantly came the cry of a gull, and then the silence had a positive quality to it. A quality of dread.

'I'm here for a specific reason,' he said. 'And your house is quite safe from me, I promise you that. In fact, my visit will end in your family having quite a bit more money than you had before—and that wouldn't come amiss, would it?'

'I—I don't care to discuss our finances with you,' she answered bleakly.

He ran his fingers through his dark, silver-streaked hair. 'God, you make it difficult, don't you?' His eyes were granite-hard. 'Prickly as a damned hedgehog——'

'And you're insulting as well,' she breathed. '*Damned* insulting. I think you'd better tell me what you've got to tell me.'

'All right, I will. I've come here from London to

39

look around your little island. And in a week or so there'll be more people coming. And we'll all be working. We're going to do a documentary programme for television, and we'll be interviewing people, going into their homes, seeing them at their fishing—or knitting—seeing your father at work on his inventions, filming your house—and using it as a base, incidentally—and when we've finished we'll go away and you'll never know we've been—until you all see yourselves on television.'

Jan had listened in growing horror to his words. And when he had finished she jumped up. 'Oh no,' she gasped. 'Oh *no*! You can't do *that*!' She had thought that nothing could be more dreadful than her father attempting to sell the house, but she had been wrong. This was worse—far worse. She looked at Breck Fallon and knew now why she had instinctively disliked him. Her feelings went deeper now. She loathed him.

'Dark Island is peaceful and right—it's just right as it is!' she burst out. 'If you come here and d-do that—it'll spoil it for ever—do you hear?' She wanted to shake him, to strike him, yet at the same moment the thought of even touching him filled her with revulsion. 'Nothing has changed here for hundreds of years—we don't want crowds of people coming here trampling over everything, leaving litter about, *spoiling* the place.'

'I assure you we're not vandals,' he said. Strange how calm he seemed. It only made greater the contrast between them. 'Nobody's going to despoil anything——'

'I mean others!' she said. 'The kind who will *watch* it on television and think "Oh, there's a pretty place, let's go there and build a house for

40

weekends"—oh, don't try and tell me anything, I've been away from here to college, I've got friends who've lived in quiet places until they went and built new roads and motorways——'

'This is different,' he cut in. 'It's off the beaten track. No motorway will ever come here——'

'We won't let you,' she said. 'When my father knows—and I'm going to tell him right now—he'll send you away——'

'He won't.' His voice stopped her in her tracks as she turned away. There was a note of certainty in it, that *knowing* tone again. 'Because he already knows why I'm here. He's already agreed. Who do you think invited me here?' Breck looked at Jan, and the dark grey eyes were like steel now, and his body was ready for swift action, like a boxer poised to fight. '*You're* the one that everybody's so frightened of. It's *you* he's worried about, which is why I timed my visit for when you'd gone to Edinburgh. So that I could be settled in when you returned. Diane told me what you'd be like, and I thought she'd exaggerated——' Diane, he had said. He knew Diane! '—but now I see she hadn't. You're so selfish and spoilt it's not true——'

Jan swung up her arm and caught him a stinging, resounding slap across his face.

There was an explosive silence for a few startled seconds, and then Breck Fallon continued: 'And far too quick-tempered.' His eyes narrowed. A muscle moved in his jaw as he went on: 'But I'll tame you before I go. If you ever do that again I'll take you over my knee and spank you!'

Two pairs of eyes met in an electric clash. For a second Jan's fingers itched to repeat her action, but something held her; the fact that she knew with

41

stone cold certainty that he was not bluffing.

'I *hate* you,' she whispered.

'Do you? I don't care about your opinion at all. You may think you're the queen of this little place —but you're not as far as I'm concerned.' He was only a foot or so away from her. Too close for comfort, but she wouldn't let him see that by moving away. 'Everyone else might jump to attention when you crack the whip, but I don't. I'm here, and I'm here to stay for a while, and you'll just have to put up with it.' He looked down at her. 'And the sooner you accept that fact the better.'

Jan couldn't speak. She turned away, picked up her racquet, and began to walk to the house. Something moved at one of the upper windows and she closed her eyes momentarily. She was going up to her bedroom and there would be a barrage of questions because either Helen or Judy had been watching and would be agog to know what had happened.

A lump burned in her throat. It was too awful to talk about, but she was going to have to tell them both who Breck Fallon was. And that he was a friend of Diane's.

'He's *not*! Oh, Jan, he can't be!' wailed Helen. 'You mean Daddy and Diane cooked this up between them? It's too ghastly for words!'

'It looks like it,' Jan answered. They were in Helen's bedroom, which overlooked the tennis court, and she crossed to the window and looked out at it. Peaceful and sunny in the morning light, and in full view. They must have wondered what was happening.

'I'm glad you hit him,' said Judy, stretched out

on the bed munching an apple. 'I'd have hit him if I'd been there. What did he say when you did it?'

'He told me he'd put me over his knee if I did it again,' Jan answered. Her head throbbed painfully. 'And he meant it.'

'Big brute!' She took a large bite out of the apple and chewed vigorously. 'It's a pity one of us isn't a boy. He needs a good *thump*. Fancy letting you think he couldn't play and then thrashing you like that—beast!'

'He's good,' said Helen. 'Let's be fair, he's a super player.'

Her two sisters stared at her. 'Whose side are you on?' Judy demanded.

'Well, ours, of course.' She went faintly pink. 'I mean, he is awful, of course, but—well, Jan did ask for it.'

'Thanks,' said Jan dryly. 'I know I did. He told me so too, in no uncertain manner.' She sat down on the bed and sighed. 'Still, that's not the main thing. The important thing is—what do we do now?'

'Go and see Daddy first,' suggested Judy. 'We can talk him out of it, perhaps?' This wistfully.

'We must. Come on, let's do it now, before *he* gets to him.' Jan stood up.

'He might be with Daddy already,' said Helen in alarm. 'He might be telling him all sorts of things——'

'Then the sooner we get in the better.' Jan opened the door. 'Come on.'

They always knocked on the door of their father's den. That was an unbroken rule they had followed since childhood. He didn't always answer, that was the only trouble. Not out of rudeness;

43

simply because he became so engrossed on the current task that he literally heard nothing of the outer world. He would go without food all day, unless reminded, and was a constant source of worry to Jan—although she never let her sisters be aware of it. He was in a way like a schoolboy who had never grown up—and she loved him dearly.

'Daddy? Are you there?' She only called this after knocking several times loudly.

There was a clatter, a muttered; 'Bother,' very mildly uttered. Cedric Sutherland had never been known to lose his temper in his life. Mild exasperation was the limit.

The door opened, and he stood there clad in a boiler suit, his grey hair untidy, glasses on the end of his nose. 'Ah!' He smiled vaguely. 'I thought I heard someone. Er—come in, do—er—all of you.'

The room was, to put it mildly, a mess. A table whose surface couldn't be seen at all for boxes, books, test tubes, racks, a bunsen burner and assorted lumps of wood and plaster and glass was the dominant piece of furniture. Two walls were lined with bulging cupboards, and he looked round and scratched his head. 'Well, sit down—if you can find anywhere. I was just working on——' he waved a hand vaguely in the direction of a fearsome-looking object near the window. It looked like a home-made boat.

'No, Daddy, it's all right,' Jan said. 'We've just come to see you about Breck.'

'*Ah!*' Slight unease filled his tone. 'Ah, him. Yes.'

'Well, I found out this morning why he's here.' Judy and Helen stood behind Jan the spokeswoman.

'Yes? I'd been meaning to talk to you about that —er—some time.' He pushed the spectacles further up his nose. In a minute they'd have dropped again. 'Only I—er—didn't get round to it, did I?'

'No, Daddy.' Jan shook her head softly. Oh, why was he so impossible to reach? He wasn't really listening now. 'You can't let him do it—the television thing, I mean. Don't you *know* what will happen?'

Her father frowned. 'Happen? I don't follow. There'll just be a couple of fellows with cameras, that's all. Nothing nasty. Just a few shots of the island and houses, and perhaps a chat to some of the people here.'

She sighed. She could see it all now, quite clearly. No doubt Diane and Breck had painted a rosy picture of this documentary, and he really believed it all. She looked round at her sisters for support, and saw two worried faces. She was, in a sense, on her own. They were little more than children themselves.

'Oh, Daddy, is that what they told you? Him and Diane? But it won't be that easy at all. This island —our home—won't be the same ever again if you let them loose here with their television cameras. Everybody will see it, and they'll want to come here—it's so beautiful, we all know that—and it'll be like—like Blackpool or Clacton!' Those were the first two names that came to her mind, and she saw the gently raised eyebrows of her father, and rushed on, before he could say anything: 'And they'll be staying *here*, won't they? Because there's nowhere else for them to stay.'

'And they'll pay us very well,' he interrupted mildly. 'And we need the money, you know that as

45

well as I.'

'Money's not everything!' That was Helen, dear loyal Helen, who had found her voice.

'No,' her father agreed gently. 'But it helps us to live.'

'We'll all work—start knitting—painting—anything,' said Jan desperately. 'But don't let them come here.'

'It's too late,' he said. 'It's already agreed. I'm sorry, my dears, but there it is. We're committed now.'

So there was nothing they could do. Breck Fallon must have known all this. He had played with her, as a cat plays with a mouse—cruelly. Jan was in her room after lunch. The scene on the tennis court came vividly back to her. He had said—what had he said? She paused in the act of dusting her dressing table, and stood there, cloth in hand. He had said: 'I'll tame you before I go.' The words brought a prickle to the back of her neck. The antagonism between them was so strong that it flowed in waves. She had not spoken to him at lunch. And he, as if sensing this too, had not spoken to her, but only to her sisters. Their father had not appeared, which was not unusual, but it had meant that the brittle atmosphere had been intensified. How I hate him, she thought, and lifted a bottle of perfume to dust underneath where it stood.

And a knock came at her door, she called: 'Come in,' and Breck Fallon walked in.

'You!' She whirled round, shocked. 'What do you want?'

'To speak to you.'

'Well, I don't want to speak to *you*,' and she turned away from him.

'I really think you had better,' he said, quite mildly, and walked across the room towards her. 'There are arrangements to be made, and you *are* the lady of the household, after all.' The words in themselves were inoffensive enough, it was the way he said them that carried a vague sense of insult.

She caught her breath. Arrangements, he said. People coming. Strangers. Then she looked at him. He was watching her, and there was nothing on his face to show his mood, but the tension was there all the same, between them, that indefinable tingle in the air that should have warned her.

'Arrangements?' She tried to keep very calm. 'You seem to have made enough already without consulting me. You seem to be doing very well on your own so far. You come here and start to turn our lives upside down——'

'Cut out the dramatics!' his voice stopped her abruptly.

'Turn your lives upside down! My God, but you do put it on. No wonder Diane warned me——' and he stopped.

'Do go on. What did Diane warn you about?'

'Forget it.' Dark grey eyes were cold, but his mouth twitched as if in amused remembrance.

'I want to *know*.' She was very tense and still.

He shrugged. 'She warned me what you'd be like —had your reaction taped exactly—so I shouldn't have been so surprised. But I thought she'd exaggerated. She hadn't. So now I'll tell you. I'm here to stay, and next week my assistant will be arriving, and after that, when we've decided on a rough plan, a camera crew will come, and your father has kindly invited us all to stay here—and there's nothing you can do about it, because no chit of a girl is going to boss *me* around or tell me what to do, so I'd advise you to get that fact straight right away and learn to live with it. It will make life a lot easier for you—and us.'

'And if I choose not to look after you?' she demanded, voice shaking.

'We'll manage. Believe me, we'll manage.'

'You're not in London now. You can't just fill a dustbin with rubbish and expect it to be emptied once a week. We have to bury or burn our waste here.' She looked him up and down. 'I shouldn't imagine you'd know where to begin.'

'I can soon learn. And Terry—my assistant—cooks better than any chef I know——' despite everything, Jan's heart gave a lurch. She prided herself on her cooking, had studied it at college, and could whip up a superb meal with the most ordinary ingredients. And yet—she tightened her lips rebelliously. No use thinking like *that*.

'I don't like anyone else in *my* kitchen,' she said firmly.

He lifted a cynical eyebrow. '*Your* kitchen? Your father's, surely?'

'I run the house, not him.'

'So now we're back to square one. Which is where I came in. My God, I'd like to shake you!'

'Touch me and see what happens,' she grated.

'I said I'd *like* to. I've no intention of doing so, believe me. You may lash out at the slightest provocation. I have a little more self-control, and I sure do need it—with you.' His eyes gleamed darkly, he stood there before her, and there was about him such an air of power that she was fright-

48

ened. Not just physical, though that was disturbing enough, but there was strength in his face, in the very set of his mouth, and eyes, and chin. Hard too. There was nothing soft about this man—not in any way. And then suddenly he smiled, and nodded. 'So now you know. I'm going.' He turned to the door. As he reached and opened it, he paused as if something else had just occurred to him. 'She was wrong about one thing, Diane. She said you were a superb cook.' He went out and closed the door quietly after him.

Jan clenched her fists in helpless anger. He was absolutely hateful! Even without that last remark, that barbed parting shot, his behaviour had been utterly arrogant. But those few words as he went out of the door had hurt—really hurt. She went to sit down on the bed and think. If this was to be a battle of wills, he seemed to be on the right path to sweeping aside any opposition effortlessly. She knew it now—knew it after seeing his face only moments previously. He was a man who would not swerve from a decision once made. 'So,' she said softly, 'what do I do now?' There was no one to answer her.

Jan sent Helen to pick as many raspberries as she could find that afternoon. There was an idea in her mind that was as yet unspoken, and to Helen's query, she merely shook her head and smiled. 'I'm making something,' she answered. The van with fresh meat came after lunch, and she debated between a beautiful chicken and a leg of pork before deciding to take both. One would go in the freezer...

Then she sent Judy to pick apples. The idea was

becoming clearer every minute. It was that remark of Breck's that had done it, but Jan was not prepared to admit it to herself yet, let alone her sisters.

She was in her element in the kitchen. Her favourite room in the house, warm and comfortable with lots of space for the many tasks she had set herself, and when she was nearly finished, she sat with her feet up and sipped a beaker of hot coffee, and gave a little smile. Someone was going to eat his words, very soon—and almost literally too.

Dressed in old jeans and check shirt, her long hair tied back with a scrap of yellow ribbon, she looked like a young teenager. She had caught a glimpse of herself in the kitchen mirror in passing. Judy's head came round the door, interrupting her in mid-thought.

'Can I come in?' she asked.

'Yes. Did you get some apples?'

'Mmm. There weren't many ripe, but I got several of the biggest.'

'Good. They'll do. Will you peel them? I'm just having a break.'

Judy sniffed. 'Gorgeous smell. What's cooking?'

Jan laughed. 'Wait and see. Until dinner.'

Judy widened her eyes. 'I thought we were going to starve him out.'

'I changed my mind. Sit down and I'll put you up to date.' She told her sister what had happened after lunch in her bedroom, and Judy listened as she peeled apples and burst out at the end:

'Oh! He's *awful!*'

'I know. But it seems as if he's won the first round. So——' Jan shrugged. 'I know when to give in gracefully. And that crack about my cooking was the last straw. So, just for a surprise, I'm going to stun him with the best dinner he's ever eaten.'

'Why?' asked Judy, who always believed in coming to the point.

Jan frowned. She could hardly admit that she didn't really know herself. 'Well,' she began, 'it's what is known as taking the enemy off guard.' It sounded quite reasonable as she said it.

'Hmm,' Judy didn't seem very impressed with that slice of logic. 'If you say so.' She stood up. 'I'll go and see how Helen's getting on with those raspberries. She's been gone ages.'

'You do that.' Jan followed suit, and stretched her arms. 'And I'll go back to slaving over my hot stove.' The aroma that came from the oven was indeed mouth-watering. She wondered briefly which soup she should serve. Busily chopping the sliced apples, sliding them into a pan, adding sugar, she thought: 'Just wait. Just you *wait*, Mr. Bighead Fallon!'

He was faintly surprised at the delicious mushroom soup, you could tell, but he said nothing. Cedric Sutherland had been persuaded to turn up for dinner on time, and he and Bréck sat talking, and Jan, on her way out to the kitchen with Helen, took a swift sidelong glance at them. She knew without any doubt that her father would have completely forgotten the morning's conversation. There would just be the vague feeling at the back of his mind that 'everything was all sorted out'. That was the way he was, and Jan wouldn't ever want him to change, not for the world.

The pork looked mouth-wateringly delicious. The apple sauce had turned out to perfection; fluffy and slightly sharp. The roast potatoes, and the peas and carrots steamed gently in their dishes, and the boat of gravy beside them looked as if it couldn't wait to be poured over all that richness.

'Will you slice the meat?' she asked Breck with a sweet smile. 'Daddy doesn't like doing it.'

'Of course.' He stood, and picking up the carving knife and fork, began to carve the joint of pork into wafer-thin succulent slices.

It really was superb. Jan had excelled herself, spurred on with the added incentive of one deliberate remark. There was silence as they ate. It was too good to spoil with conversation, and Helen looked up, caught Jan's eye, and winked.

Breck did his plate justice, she had to admit that. She would have disliked him more if he had been a fussy eater. But he wasn't, and when his plate was empty he looked up, and his eyes met Jan's. The spark was there, but it was unreadable.

'More—Breck?' She had to force his name out.

'I couldn't. But it was absolutely delicious.'

'Was it? I'm so glad.' She stood up. 'I hope you have room for the sweet?' She started stacking plates and Breck rose.

'Let me help you.' He didn't wait for her reply, but picked up a pile of plates and cutlery and followed her out.

'You really shouldn't have bothered,' she spoke without turning round on her way along the passage to the kitchen. 'My sisters are used to it.'

'No bother. I couldn't sit there and allow myself to be waited on.' He reached a long arm out to push open the door for her, and Jan sailed in. For some absurd reason, she felt happy. It was a *satisfied* feeling.

'Leave them on the table. Please,' she added as

an afterthought. The raspberry mousse was ready on the table, already set out in five dishes, topped with cream and a cherry. She saw his eyes on the dishes, and smiled slightly.

'Raspberry mousse—I hope you're not allergic to them or anything.'

He was still looking, then he tore his eyes away. 'Did you make them?' he asked.

'Of course.' She could meet his glance very coolly, which helped. 'Are you surprised?'

He shook his head. Surely he wasn't lost for words? she wondered in amusement.

'No—no.'

'Good. Perhaps you'll be kind enough to carry them in on that tray. I'll pour out the coffee.' And she turned away and went over to the bubbling coffee pot.

'I'll take in the coffee instead if you like. The cups will be more difficult.' Was he actually trying to be helpful? She bit back a laugh that threatened to escape. 'As you wish. It won't be a moment.'

She thought he was still at the table. her back stiffened in surprise as his voice came from just behind her shoulder. 'Why?' he asked. He was getting like Judy.

She turned slowly round. 'I beg your pardon. Why what?'

'You know damn well. I've just been served with a meal that wouldn't have been out of place at the Savoy. And that mousse looks like it floated in from heaven.'

'You do have a poetic way of expressing yourself,' she answered. 'Perhaps it's your job. I really don't know what you mean. Are you being sarcastic or something?'

He took a deep breath. 'Give me strength! Sarcastic! You know you excelled yourself this evening. Why the contrast?'

She lifted one eyebrow. 'Thank you for the rather backhanded compliment. Why, I just enjoy cooking—and today I felt inspired, that's all. I'm *so* glad you enjoyed your dinner.' The coffee was bubbling in the percolator, and she turned away from him and lifted it from the heat.

'Excuse me, I must pour it out while it's nice and hot. Would you put some milk into that brown jug on the table, please?'

'Yes. Can you manage the coffee?'

'I can, thank you.' It was happening again—the brittle tension that grew whenever they were alone together in the same place. She could feel it; was as aware of it as of the heat from the percolator she held. A breathless tautness that stretched between them in an almost tangible way, making her heart beat faster. She had been so calm only minutes before, now she felt confused. And the fact that she knew he was watching her made it worse. For he was regarding her, quite coolly, as she poured out the hot black coffee.

'Incredible,' he murmured softly.

She took a deep breath. 'What is?'

'Not what—*who*. You.'

She turned too sharply, because there was something in his voice that had stung her, and as a result the coffee spilled over on to the table top. A rich hot pool of brown spread instantly, and Jan instinctively jerked her hand back.

He was there, instantly. Taking the pot out of her hand, saying:

'Have you scalded yourself?'

'No.' Funny, she could have sworn there was concern in his voice. 'But what a *mess*!'

'It won't take a second to clear up. Where's a cloth?'

'In the sink.'

'Right. Move that cup out of the way.' He had the cloth, he began wiping up the spilt coffee, and Jan obeyed him wordlessly. There was something so decisive about his actions that she would have been foolish to oppose them. The tension had gone, evaporated with the spilt coffee. It would return later, that was inevitable, but just for the moment it was no longer there.

'Okay, all done.' He squeezed the dishcloth out, rinsed it and spread it to dry on the draining board. 'I'll finish pouring. There's enough left in the pot. You take in that mousse. I'll follow.'

It was not until she was in the dining room that Jan realized what had happened. She had allowed Breck Fallon to order her about. Reasonably enough under the circumstances—but vaguely disturbing. No one had ever done that before.

She saw Judy's cynical expression as he came in a few moments later with the coffee, but there was nothing she could say. It would have to be later. She had completely forgotten the reason for the accident. That too would return later. All she knew was one thing. She wished it were anyone but *him* who had come to alter their lives so drastically. She was in a turmoil of muddled emotions regarding him. On the one hand aggressive, arrogant, rude—and on the other, decisive, clearly highly intelligent—and utterly puzzling—all wrapped up in one package that was called Breck Fallon. And he had warned her quite clearly of his intentions. Jan drank her coffee and watched him talking to her father. Courteous and quietly spoken, he seemed a different man again, darkly handsome in his own hawklike way; she suddenly realized something she should have done before now. He was a devastatingly attractive animal.

CHAPTER FOUR

JAN rose early the next morning. It was a relief to get out of bed after a restless night of muddled dreams. It was nearly six, and the grey mist which shrouded the house and clung wetly to the windows matched her mood. The silent house slept, and she walked quietly about the kitchen in her slippers and warm dressing gown and put the kettle on the stove for a refreshing cup of tea.

She looked at the working surface beside the cooker. It was there that it had happened, the previous evening. And she knew suddenly what was bothering her. Their mother had died seven years previously, when Jan had been fourteen and her elder sister Diane was twenty. But it was Jan who had taken upon herself the virtual running of the house from that time, except for two years away at college. Jan who had sorted everything out, Jan the capable. Her family had come to her with their problems, and she had been the one who was there, making the decisions, coping with the many tasks that constantly needed doing. She was used to it, and would not have it any other way. And yet that previous night, when Breck had calmly and decisively told her what to do, she had meekly obeyed. A strange new sensation—but not unpleasant, that was the thing that had made her uneasy. And now it was admitted, she felt the better for it, and the restless dreams that had plagued her sleep slipped into perspective.

She poured boiling water into the teapot and put the lid on and went to the refrigerator for milk. And Breck Fallon walked into the kitchen and said: 'Ah, it's you.'

She put the milk jug down first. There would be no repetition of that stupid accident. 'You!' she exclaimed. 'What are you doing up?'

'Lovely welcome.' His tone was dry. 'It's not six yet. I heard noises—my room's directly over this—and I thought it was burglars.'

'And you came down to investigate?'

'I did. I could hardly lie there and let someone rifle the house, could I?'

'We don't have burglars on Dark Island. We haven't even got a policeman.'

'Ah, but I didn't know that, did I?'

'Would you like a cup of tea? I've just made one.' She didn't know why she asked that.

'Yes, please.' He sat down at the table and watched her fetch another beaker. He had taken time to dress in jeans and an unbuttoned jacket, although underneath that was a bare hairy chest. She wondered—very briefly, of course—if he slept naked. She had not heard a sound, not even of him coming along the corridor, and the boards always creaked.

'You move quietly,' she said, pouring milk into the beakers. 'I heard nothing.'

A slight smile. 'No sense in warning a housebreaker. Surprise is a big factor in catching them.'

Despite herself, she was intrigued. '*Them?* Did you expect more than one—and you still crept down?'

'I didn't think you'd appreciate me coming in to ask you to hold my hand while I came down—your screams would, I'm sure, have scared the hardiest cat burglar off. So I decided to go it alone, yes.'

The veiled arrogance in his tone, only slightly hidden by amusement, stung her to retort: 'And you weren't nervous?'

'No. Should I be?'

'Most men would be.' It was a ridiculous conversation to be having, but she couldn't help herself. She was embarrassed by his near-nakedness, his aggressive maleness, which communicated itself to her even more overtly at this early hour of the morning, and felt the absurd need to keep talking. He shook his head faintly, as if surprised. 'If I saw a loaded shotgun pointed at me, I assure you I'd do exactly as I was told—failing that, I'd wade in and sort it all out in a few minutes.'

He didn't even sound conceited—just matter-of-fact, that was the annoying thing. The tea was brewed. She poured it out and pushed the sugar bowl towards him.

'You're either very brave—or very foolish,' was all she could think of to say. Breck gently pushed the bowl towards her again.

'No sugar, thanks. Neither, actually. But I know enough about unarmed combat to look after myself, that's all.' He lifted his beaker, took a swallow, and nearly choked. 'My God! What's this?'

Jan had not bothered to switch on the light. She could see well enough, although the room was a bit grey in the misty morning light. She took a sip from her own beaker and felt a wave of humiliation:

'I forgot—I must have forgotten to put the tea in the p-pot,' she said weakly.

And he began to laugh. 'Beautiful! Well

brewed water and milk! Come on, let's put the kettle on again. It won't take a minute.' He stood and went to the cooker, still laughing, and Jan, furious now, jumped up and caught his arm.

'*I'll* do it—*thank you*! You go and l-laugh to yourself.' Her voice caught with a mixture of mortification and anger, and she realized that her hand was still on his arm and took it away as though it burnt her—which, in a funny way, it did.

Breck turned and put his own hands on her arms. 'Ah-ah! Temper!' His smile was a white blur in the shadowy room. 'Just calm down, little hedgehog. It could happen to anyone. Now sit down, and I'll make the *tea*.' But his voice still shook with hidden laughter.

Jan, incensed, lifted her hands to try and free herself from his grip, which immediately tightened as he whispered: 'And don't try and fight me—you couldn't win in a million years.'

'Oh, couldn't I?' She stamped on his bare foot and twisted her body violently away. It was an action she regretted instantly, for not only was she not free, but she was now held in a grip of steel. Utterly helpless. 'Let me *go*,' she breathed, panic rising.

'When I'm ready. I'll teach you to kick my foot, you bad-tempered little witch.' The hold tightened imperceptibly, she felt his warm breath on her cheek, then near her mouth, nearer—and then his lips were on hers.

Her heart thudded violently against her chest, her arms were weak, her body limp, completely helpless against his own warm body as his mouth burned hers into submission with a deep kiss that went on and on...

And then he released her so suddenly that she would have fallen had he not reached immediately to hold her arms.

'You are hateful!' she managed to whisper, frightened because she felt weak and dizzy. 'You're a bully—a horrible bully——'

'Oh yes, I'm that all right. So just remember when you feel like doing a bit of bullying yourself —you'll have your work cut out with me—I don't take lightly to being trodden on by a kid like you——'

'Kid?' she gasped. 'You didn't *kiss* me as though I was a kid.'

He reached up to stroke her cheek, and laughed softly. 'That was just a sample. I must admit I'd have probably got more response from a statue— but we can't have everything in life, can we?' He patted her cheek. 'So long, *kid*. I'll do without the tea. Be careful how you pour it out—and try not to forget the tea-bags this time.'

He turned and padded silently out, closing the door after him equally quietly.

Jan put her hand to her mouth. She was trembling all over. Humiliation filled her, but mixed with it was an odd stirring of excitement. She didn't understand it herself, but she knew she needed that cup of tea, now more than ever. She lit the gas under the kettle—but only after wasting three matches.

It was something she could not tell her sisters. She could tell no one. An implacable loathing for Breck Fallon now filled her with an intensity that was dismaying because it coloured all her thoughts for the rest of the day, and caused her to make mistakes in her many tasks.

There was one job that had needed doing for weeks, and she had kept putting it off. But the morning's mist was the decisive factor, and the job could no longer be left, for the damp still clung to the outside windows, and they were, she told herself, a disgrace.

Helen saw her searching out bucket and cloths after breakfast, and said: 'I'll do the downstairs windows if you like.'

'Will you, love?' Jan straightened up from the sink. 'Here's a cloth for you, then. We'll go round the same way, then the one bucket will do.' She felt that if she worked hard, really hard, she wouldn't have time to think about that man. Her father had locked himself in his den after breakfast and that was the last they would see of him all day, and Breck had gone off walking after the meal, at which he had behaved with a grave courtesy to Jan that had only left her feeling more confused than ever. The kiss might never have been. In fact at one point, as she looked across the table at him, Jan wondered if she could have imagined it. But she knew a second later that she hadn't, when he turned, caught her eye, and she saw the dark gleam of mockery there.

She looked away quickly, but the memory of that brief expression lingered even now as she filled the bucket with hot water and added a dash of ammonia. It was heavy to carry.

'You're very quiet,' remarked Helen as they went outside to where a watery sun had managed to poke its head through damp clouds. 'Has he done anything?'

'What makes you say that?' asked Jan sharply.

'Don't jump down my throat!' Helen laughed. 'I only asked. It usually is him now.'

'Huh! I don't give a fig for *him*,' answered Jan, putting the bucket down with a clatter on to the cobblestones outside the back door.

'No, I can see you don't. Still, he is quite good-looking in a sort of dark sexy way, isn't he?'

Jan looked at her sister in dismay. 'I hope Judy never hears you,' she commented, trying to sound terribly casual—but not sure if she was succeeding.

Helen's look was quite a shrewd one. 'You know *her*. She can't stand men. 'Course I wouldn't tell her, she'd bite my head off. But I can say it to you, can't I? I mean, we know *why* he's here now—at least he's not buying our home—that's the most important thing to me—and I suppose we'll get used to the idea of cameras and things——'

'*I* won't,' said Jan firmly. 'I don't care how much they pay, it's not worth it. I'm surprised at Diane for putting the idea into his head, as she obviously did. It's all right for her, living in London—she never was one for island life—I mean she couldn't wait to get away as soon as she was old enough— but you'd have thought she'd think what it would do to our lives.' She sighed and bent to wring out the chamois leather cloth in the warm water, and she didn't see Helen's expression. If she had, she would have wondered at it.

The ladder was propped against an outhouse, and Jan hefted it and set it by the back door. The first window she cleaned would be to Breck's bedroom. Helen had already begun cleaning the kitchen window when she reached it. Steadying herself with one hand on the ledge, she began to wipe the glass. There was a satisfaction in hard work, she knew. Full of boundless energy, Jan had never relished being idle, and although she enjoyed reading, could not sit still to do so for more than an hour without wanting to be up and away and doing again.

Now she busily cleaned the windows until they sparkled, and moved gradually round the house, working in perfect time with Helen. They both sang as they worked, two young voices raised in tuneful harmony as they progressed through 'The Skye Boat Song' to 'Amazing Grace' and on to a particular favourite of them both, 'Lord of the Dance'.

And it was as they were half way through this that disaster struck. Busily singing and wiping away, Jan had been only slightly aware that there was a very faint wobble to the ladder, but had ignored it, being too engrossed in her twin tasks. And then she leaned just that bit further to clean the left top corner of the window, put out her left hand to steady herself on the windowsill—and a portion of stone crumbled away as she did so. She felt herself going—a most terrifying sensation, heard a distant scream—and further away, a man's shout, but all this was swallowed up in a dizzying arc as she and the ladder went sideways and down, parting company at the ground as she thudded into a flower bed full of prickly roses.

She lay there dazed, heard Helen's sobbing voice through a blurry haze: 'Jan, oh, Jan love—are you all right?'

She ached. All over. 'Helen——' she began, in a whisper, and managed to open her eyes, almost fearful of what she might see. Her head ached too, and she couldn't move. That was the most frighten-

ing thing. She could not *move*. 'Helen—help
me——'

'Jan, lie still. Don't try to move. I'm going to lift
you.' She couldn't understand it. That wasn't
Helen. Breck's face swam into view—and he wasn't
laughing at her.

It was the first time she had been glad to see him.
'I *can't* move,' she burst out.

'Only because you've got about ten thousand
rose thorns stuck in your clothes—and possibly in
you.' He knelt; now he was easing his hand under
her shoulder and knees.

'Don't worry, I won't hurt you, I promise—only
we must get you out of this mess first.' Then she
was being lifted, oh, so gently, and she heard—and
felt, the snapping of dozens of threads in her
clothes as he did so.

'Helen,' he spoke briskly. 'Go and heat water
and find some antiseptic. Take it into Jan's bedroom.' He turned to Jan, lying helplessly in his
arms. 'Have I hurt you at all?'

'No,' a faint croak, then she winced.

'Where *do* you hurt?'

'My—my right arm and—I think—my left foot.
I'm not sure.'

'All right, don't talk now. You'll soon be all
right. Now, I'm going to carry you up to your bedroom, and I'll take it slowly, but you tell me the
second anything I do bothers you. Okay?'

'Yes,' she whispered. She closed her eyes. He
moved lightly, easily—gently. She was hardly
aware of movement, only vaguely, but then he
said:

'Open your eyes, Jan.' She did so. They were in
her bedroom.

'I'm going to lay you down on your bed. I'll do it very carefully. Then I'll leave you while Helen gets all those rose thorns away and cleans you with antiseptic. You'll have to get all your clothes off. Do you hear me?'

'Yes.' She could hear Helen coming up the stairs as he eased her on to the red candlewick bedspread. He repeated his words to Helen as she came in, and she nodded, wide-eyed.

'Yes, Breck. Right away.'

He closed the door after him, and the next quarter of an hour was spent in removing all the painful thorns, dabbing the tiny wounds with antiseptic, and then redressing Jan in a clean pair of jeans and shirt from her drawer. Helen bundled up the clothes Jan had been wearing, and grimaced. 'I'll give these a good going over before I wash them,' she said. 'Though they're nearly ruined.'

Jan lay back, white-faced and exhausted. 'It's a good job I landed in those roses,' she said slowly. 'I could have been killed anywhere else.'

Helen sobered. 'I know. Oh, Jan, let me get you some brandy or whisky or something. You look terrible.'

Jan managed a faint grin. 'So do you. You'd better——' she stopped as the knock came on the door, and then Breck's voice:

'Have you finished?'

Helen opened the door. 'Come in. Yes, I was just telling Jan she needed a drink.'

'Yes. Tea—or coffee. Off you go.' He turned to Jan. 'I'm going to have a look at you, and before you say anything, my father is a doctor, so's my mother, and I've probably got as much knowledge as a third-year medical student, so are you going to

66

trust me, or do you want me to go and bring a doctor?'

'There isn't one,' she whispered. 'Only on the mainland. I'll—trust you.' She lifted her head from the pillow. 'It's only my arm and ankle. The rest of me is just like a pincushion, but that's all.'

'I know, I'm sorry—but that flower bed probably saved you from serious injury.' His hands were cool and precise as he deftly held her foot and felt round her ankle. 'Hmm. Without an X-ray it's impossible to tell, of course—but I honestly think it's a bad sprain.' He held the ball of her foot. 'Wriggle your toes if you can.' She did so. 'Will you let me strap it up for you?'

'Yes.' It was strange, but she trusted him completely. 'Why aren't you a doctor too?'

One corner of his mouth lifted in a slight smile. 'Because I preferred the bright lights of London—and television—but we won't go into that now. You've got to keep calm, and you won't if we argue.' But there was none of the usual aggression in his voice. 'Where's your first aid box?'

'In a corner of the bathroom—under the stool.'

'All right, let me see your arm first.' She could see the bruise for herself, near the elbow. It would be enormous soon. But she could move her arm easily although the skin was sore because of a long red graze from elbow to wrist.

'A nice sight—but it'll be fine in a couple of days if you have good healing flesh. I'll go and find that box now. Won't be a minute.'

She had a question to ask him, and when he came back, carrying a large biscuit tin that was always kept crammed full of essentials, she said: 'Why were you so near when I fell—had you just

67

returned?'

'Yes—and no.' He was busy setting out bandages, plaster and scissors on her bedside table. 'I was on my way back, and I stopped to listen to the two of you singing. You wouldn't have been able to see me, I was by the thick trees. Then I saw the stone-work give way and ran forward—I could see what was going to happen. Unfortunately I wasn't in time. I'm sorry.'

So that had been the shout she had heard. Faintly, and mingling with Helen's scream; Breck running forward to try and save her falling. She felt suddenly very tired. 'I was stupid,' she began. 'I knew the ladder wasn't very steady. But I wanted to finish——' her voice tailed away.

'I know. Don't try and talk if you don't want to. Accidents happen. Just try and relax. This may hurt a little, but I'll try not to.'

Jan lay back, and he began to strap her ankle up with crêpe bandage. Tightly and firmly, and already it felt better. He didn't hurt her at all.

'Tea,' Helen's voice came from the doorway, and she walked in with three beakers on a tray.

Breck came round beside Jan. 'I'll lift you up,' he said. 'I'll do your arm afterwards.' Helen stood solemnly looking at Jan's foot.

'Is it very bad?' she asked Breck with wide eyes.

'No. It'll be fine in less than a week——'

'Oh!' Jan exclaimed as Breck eased her into a sitting position.

'Have I hurt you?' he asked quickly.

'No, but I can't—there's so many things to *do*,' she began.

'They'll just have to wait. You're staying here for a day or two——'

'Oh, *no*, I can't! I must——' she began to struggle from the bed and he leaned over and stopped her.

'Hold it. Where do you think you're going?'

'I'm going to try and *walk*, what else?' she looked at him defiantly.

'No, you're not. Here, drink this.' He handed her the tea. 'That should keep you quiet for a moment. Now let's get this straight.' He took his beaker from the waiting Helen. 'Thanks. *You* are not going anywhere. Not in that state. Apart from anything else, you're suffering from shock. Your right arm is badly bruised and you won't be able to use it for a few days, ditto your ankle—which will not improve if you insist on walking round.'

Jan swallowed some tea. She felt a little better immediately. 'I'm strong,' she said. 'I'll manage.'

'You must be to have recovered so well,' he admitted. 'Drink some more tea—it's obviously doing you good.'

She did so. She was beginning to remember certain things that the accident had pushed to the back of her mind. Things like a kiss, and the way he had held her, and told her what he thought of her, only hours before. And one thing was sure, she wasn't taking orders from *him*. He had called her a kid. That still rankled.

'Helen,' she said, 'will you go down and make me a sandwich or get a couple of biscuits? I'm starving.' She waited until she had gone out, then said: 'Thank you for all you've done, but I'll be fine in half an hour or so. And you can't tell me what to do—any more than I can tell *you*.'

He sat down beside her on the bed. 'You know,' he said, 'I've never met anyone like you before. I honestly thought you were a hospital case when I saw you stretched out on the ground—and here you are half an hour later giving your orders again. You're incredible!'

'You said that last night,' she replied swiftly. 'And I remember what happened. I can also remember what happened this morning—so please don't start another argument.'

'*Me?*' The wide mouth curved. 'My God, I don't believe it!' He leaned forward and put his hand to his forehead, and his body was shaking. Then she saw why. It was with silent laughter.

'Get *off* my bed!' she said.

He stood up, sobering quickly. 'Okay, you're fine. Let's do your arm. Then we'll see how well you walk.'

She thought that he might take satisfaction in hurting her when he bandaged her arm, but she was surprised at how carefully he did so.

Helen returned with two chocolate digestive biscuits on a plate, and Jan ate them, then looked at Breck.

'Right. May I walk now?' she asked him. She had every intention of doing so whatever his answer.

He shrugged. 'You'll try anyway,' he answered. 'So it might as well be while I'm here—to catch you.' The last three words very softly spoken.

Jan gritted her teeth and swung her legs from the bed. She took a deep breath, then stood up. At least she could do that. Tentatively she put her left foot forward, and pain shot through her ankle like a white-hot knitting needle being twisted inside it. The room wavered, she moved her right leg forward and the agony of standing on her left foot was nearly unbearable, but she began to breathe deeply, if only to stop herself from crying out in pain. Her forehead was damp with perspiration, and there was a buzzing in her ears that grew louder—and louder ...

'All right, that's it. Admit defeat.' Breck's arms came round her at the same moment as she heard his words. It was as well they did, for Jan was unable to stop herself from falling backwards into the great black void that had opened in the floor ...

CHAPTER FIVE

'It's all organized. Are you listening, Jan?' Helen's voice penetrated her brain, and Jan opened her eyes to see her sister sitting on the edge of the bed. Of Breck there was no sign. Breck... She must have fainted.

She sat up. 'What happened?'

'You passed out very gracefully and he caught you and hefted you on the bed again. He told me to stay with you a while, and just keep talking to you. You'd come round sooner that way, he said.'

'Oh. What were you saying? What's all organized?'

'Oh well, he knew you were worried about work and cooking and everything, so he's gone to phone this Terry person—the one who's his assistant, and he's a good cook—and see if he can come tomorrow instead of Monday. And Judy and I will do the meals today, and Breck will finish cleaning the windows, he says, so you're not to worry about a *thing*.'

'Oh, I see.' But she felt uneasy. There was nothing she could put her finger on, but she felt worried and restless. 'What time is it now?'

'Nearly half past eleven. You've been asleep for about half an hour.'

'Me? Asleep? Never!'

'You have, honest. He said you must be very tired, with the shock, you know, and it would do you good, if you wanted to sleep. So I've been chattering away while you've been snoring your head off.'

Her ankle throbbed when she tried to move it and Jan winced. And her arm was stiff and very sore. All of a sudden she felt like crying. 'Helen,' she said. 'What are we going to *do*?'

'About what?' Her sister looked puzzled.

'About *him*. Breck, of course. He's *awful*—he's taking over.'

Helen smiled. 'You're poorly, that's all. He said you might be a bit depressed when you came round. I think he's behaved very well.'

Jan looked at her thoughtfully. It was not her imagination. Little things that Helen had said, when you pieced them all together, started to add up. The girl was not as averse to Breck as she should be.

She opened her mouth to ask her—and Breck was standing in the doorway. Had he heard anything? 'I've been through to London on the phone,' he said, 'and it's all fixed.' Helen muttered something that sounded like: 'I'll go and find Judy,' and vanished. Panic filled Jan.

'What is?'

'Didn't Helen tell you? Terry—my assistant will come tomorrow and do all the cooking until you're better. So that's one worry off your mind.' He smiled almost kindly. 'It's painful trying to get through by phone to anywhere from here. I don't know how you stand it. Are you feeling better?'

'Yes, thank you. And I like the phone the way it is. We don't need all your modern contraptions to keep us going,' she answered.

He raised his eyebrows. 'Oh dear, have I started something again? We don't seem able to have a decent conversation, do we?'

'No, we don't. But then our worlds are so far apart, aren't they?' she answered. 'We don't *want* to be up to date here. Our way of life hasn't changed—but it's a damn good one.'

'Which is why you don't have television?'

'Yes.'

'Then why,' he said slowly, and, she could have sworn, with a certain relish, 'do you have a freezer, a washer, and vacuum cleaner?'

'Because——' Damn the man! 'Because they don't intrude on our lives like television would. They're quiet—and useful. *You* wouldn't understand, being a man.'

'Ah! The eternal feminine logic—I, as a mere male, wouldn't understand. There's no answer to that, is there? I may understand rather better than you imagine.' Yet his face was inscrutable; dark and strong; he seemed to be waiting for something —she knew not what. She moved uneasily on the bed, wanting him to go away, to plan what she had to do next.

'I'm tired,' she said.

'No, you're not. You've just had a doze—which I gather is unheard of——' Helen had been talking, that was obvious. 'So now you're full of beans and ready to take charge again, aren't you?' He moved slightly on the bed. His sleeves were rolled nearly to the elbow and she noticed for the first time that dozens of tiny scratches covered his forearms. 'Just because you've lost a point in our eternal battle you think you'll call it quits.'

'Nonsense. You've hurt your arms. Have you put ointment on?'

'Don't change the subject.' But he looked down

74

in faint surprise. 'So I have. I never noticed. That would be when I lifted you out of your prickly bed of roses.'

'You'd better put something on now, from the first aid box. I'd hate to be responsible for you getting tetanus or anything.'

He gave her a crooked little smile. 'I'll bet you would! All right, bossy, I'll do it now.' He stood and went over to the box and rummaged through. Then, casually he said: 'Didn't you have a terrible struggle with your conscience?'

'What with?'

'The phone—freezer—cleaner—anything new-fangled.'

'No. Go *away*.' She lay back, and he began to laugh.

'You're not doing it right. You should close your eyes, look a bit more pale and fragile, and say "go away" in a very faint voice.'

'You are impossible!'

'So are you.' He sat down on the side of the bed again, and began to smear antiseptic cream on his many scratches. 'I've already told you, you can't boss me around—you couldn't before, you're certainly not going to now. And the sooner you get that into your pretty little head, the better it will be for you.' Cool grey eyes met hers in a long challenging glance. 'Because, for the next few days, you're going to be dependent on me. You won't like that, but you'll just have to swallow your pride and accept it.'

'What—what do you mean?'

'I mean that I'll have to carry you around, unless you want to stay up here and read—and I don't think that will appeal.'

'*You*—carry *me* around!'

'Yes. You certainly can't walk. Think what a hell of a mess you'd be in if I wasn't here.'

'I wouldn't be in this mess if you weren't here, let's get that clear. The windows could have waited a while longer—but knowing *hordes* of strangers were going to descend on us—well, I had to do something.' Jan's eyes sparkled, her cheeks were faintly pink with the effort of putting *him* straight. If he thought he was going to get away with anything . . .

'Come on now! "Hordes" of strangers. About four, and I'll guarantee their good behaviour right *now*. You'll scarcely notice they're here at all, I promise you that.'

'Huh! And anyway, I'd manage somehow, don't worry. Judy and Helen would help me to get about.'

'I gather they have enough jobs of their own to do, without nursing you.'

'And haven't you? You are here to work too, aren't you?'

'So I am. But my hours are pretty flexible. I'll sort it all out somehow.'

'Oh, I'm sure you will.' She lay back wearily. The conversation was tiring her more than she cared to admit. And she was having to do some mental readjustment. Useless to keep on fighting. She was in a way completely helpless. But no man had ever told her what to do before, and it was against her nature to accept defeat—but apparently she had no choice. None at all.

'It's difficult for you, isn't it?' Was he a mind-reader? It was as if he *knew*. But in a strange way, it decided her.

'Not difficult at all,' and she even managed to smile as she said it. 'Will you please help me downstairs now? To the kitchen? Then I'll get lunch sorted out with one of my sisters.'

'I'll take you to to the kitchen, but lunch is already taken good care of—while you were sleeping I took the liberty of having a look around there. I hope you enjoy your meal.'

She stared at him. 'You—what have you done?'

'Why not let it be a surprise? Don't look so horrified. You'll like it. And while we're on the subject of food, I'm going to mention another thing that seems to fill you with horror—only now you're a captive audience. Namely, money. We have to come to some agreement about payment now. Do you have a bank account?'

She looked at him. 'No.'

'I thought not. Is there a post office on this island?'

'Well, sort of—but it's very tiny. Why?'

'Because we could arrange payment through there. Or would you prefer cash?'

'That would be best.' She didn't like him talking about it. 'Wouldn't it be better for you to see my father?'

'Probably, but I tried once, when I first came, and he is, if possible, worse than you—if you'll forgive me saying so.'

She knew what he meant. She couldn't help the smile after that. 'Yes, he would be. Daddy is very vague.' She sighed.

'Look, you're in no fit state to worry your head. Terry and I will organize something when he comes. As long as you'll leave it to me. Will you?'

'I suppose so.'

'Right. Are you ready to move?'

As he carried her downstairs, she couldn't help asking, although she hated herself for doing so: 'How much will we get, roughly?'

He told her—and she clutched him in stunned disbelief. It was an amount she couldn't even imagine.

'How much?' She couldn't have heard aright.

He repeated the figure. And there was no mistake. There was silence until he helped her on to a chair in the kitchen, which was empty, and she looked at him wide-eyed.

'I don't believe it,' she said faintly.

'Don't you? It's true. We'll claim for our board at hotel rates, then there's the trouble and bother of using your home—and filming here, keeping this as our base while we go all over the island. Do you have a boat?'

'Yes. But——'

'If you'll let us borrow that too, you'll get more.'

'I don't believe it,' she repeated, even more faintly.

'Don't try. Look, can I get you a cup of tea or anything?'

'Yes, please. Tea caddy's over there.'

She watched him take it. The kitchen was filled with pleasantly rich aroma of something cooking in the oven. Not recognizable as yet, but promising to be interesting.

Her mind raced ahead. She would be able to buy those curtains now without the enormous worry of juggling the budget. There would be money to do all the essential jobs that had just been put off and put off because there was nothing to cover them.

And more—much more, for months and months ahead ...

'It's not right,' she said.

He looked round from the cooker. 'What?'

'I said it's not right. We can't take that much. It wouldn't be'—she struggled to find a word—'correct.'

He put the teapot on the table with a thud. 'Don't start again!'

'Start? I'm not starting anything. I'm just *telling* you.'

'Well, *don't*. I've never met a woman like you before who could so——'

'Well, that makes two of us. Because I've never met a man like *you*!'

It was no use. The truce was clearly over, if it had ever existed. The crackling tension filled the room again. And the eyes of Jan and Breck met in a silent, startling clash. The big powerful man with the dark grey eyes and manner that could switch with startling speed from gentleness to aggression; and Jan slender and dark and at the moment quite helpless—physically but not mentally. She would not look away—she would *not*.

Then he began to smile—slowly. 'My God,' he said softly. 'But you're one on your own. You really are.'

'Do you think you have the right to speak to me as you like?'

'Have I called you names?'

'No. But you're rude and aggressive. We don't all consider money to be the most important thing in the world, you know.'

'I'm beginning to realize that, believe me. And what makes you think I do?'

'You thought the mention of all that money would overwhelm me.'

'You nearly fell out of my arms when I said it,' he pointed out logically. 'So you can't pretend to be entirely unmoved.'

'It was a surprise, that's all.'

'You soon got over it.'

'Yes, I did. And I don't *care* about your opinion of money. Not at all. I'm just telling you mine.'

'So you've told me. Duly noted and taken down. Here, drink your tea.' He pushed a beaker across the table to her.

Helen and Judy walked into the kitchen from the back door. Helen carried an armful of roses, and Judy a basket of apples.

'Are you better, Jan?' Judy went quickly over to her. 'Helen told me what happened.' She spared Breck a brief glance that implied that it was probably all his fault anyway. 'How awful!'

'Yes, I'm much better, thanks. I'll have to rest my ankle for a couple of days, but then I'll be okay.' She peered at the apples. 'Why all these?'

Breck spoke before Judy had a chance. 'I asked her to pick plenty. Helen said she'd help me make a few apple pies for the weekend. Do you mind?'

Jan shrugged, and looked at Judy. They would have to have a talk later. 'It's all right. There are thousands. If your friend is coming tomorrow, you'd better both go and get a room ready.'

Helen dumped the roses by the sink. 'I'll put these in water after. Come on, Judy.'

There was silence for a few moments after they had gone, then Jan spoke. 'Do you know how to make pastry?' she asked him.

'No. But I'll learn. Got a book?'

'No. But I'll tell you.' And she smiled slowly. 'It might be interesting to see how you manage.'

'Yes, it might. I'm looking forward to it, actually.'

'Then why not begin now? I'll do the apples—you can make the pastry.'

'Tell me what I'll need first. I am in your hands entirely.' Tinged with mockery, his voice left her in no doubt that he appreciated the subtle irony of the situation.

She felt herself go pink, and to cover up, said quickly: 'The table needs a good wipe down first. There's a mixing bowl and pastry board over there...'

Everything was ready at last. Hands scrubbed clean, Breck rolled out his newly made pastry with all the authority of a born cook. His cheek was smudged with flour, and his arms were covered with it, and one eyebrow had turned white, as if in surprise, but Jan knew that he was enjoying himself. A strange sensation filled her, and she had to take a deep breath. She didn't understand why she should suddenly feel so breathless, nor why her heart should have thudded as it did. She looked away, and Breck said:

'Am I doing it right?'

She swallowed. 'Yes. Fine—not too thin with that piece. That's enough.'

'Now what?'

'Get the pie dish and lay that piece in it—carefully now. Right, now cut round the edges with your knife.'

Fifteen minutes later, three spicy apple pies—gently sprinkled with cinnamon—were put into the oven, and Breck carefully removed the casserole dish and put it on top. 'I'm going to do some rice now,' he said. 'I've curried the pork that was left from last night. Helen told me you all liked a mild curry.'

'We do.'

He grinned boyishly—made more so with the flour on his face. 'Good. It's my speciality. Let's see what the expert makes of my efforts.'

Jan sat back. Her ankle ached, her arm hurt, and she suddenly wanted nothing so much as to be comforted by someone—and looked after. Her eyes filled with tears she could not help, and she blinked furiously.

'It's not *that* bad, is it?' He was watching her.

'What? No, it's——' her voice trembled. 'Oh! Just leave me alone,' sniffing, she fumbled desperately for her handkerchief. 'Oh damn!'

'Here.' A clean white one was pushed into her hand. 'I think you'd better go and lie down. I'll send your lunch up.'

'No, you won't.' She blew her nose furiously after wiping the treacherous tears away. 'I'm all right.'

'No, you're damn well not. Little idiot! Come on.' He put his arms round her waist, to lift her, and Jan pushed out angrily, feebly.

'Leave me alone, you—you——' But his arms were warm and oddly comforting, considering that she loathed him, and he was too strong to be pushed away, and she was standing there, and he was just holding her, and it was very nice, very nice ... Horrified, Jan jerked upright, because she had been leaning on him. She could scarcely breathe, her heart thudded uncontrollably, and her legs were very weak.

'All right. It's all right, don't struggle. You're a game little fighter, but you can't go on for ever, you know. Take it easy, Jan.' The words were soothing and calming.

'No—you mustn't touch me——' she gasped. 'Leave me alone——'

'Don't fight me. It's no use. Come on, I'll take you into the living room. I'll find you a pile of books and you can sit and relax.'

'No. There's a whole lot of washing to be done——'

'The heck with the washing. The house won't fall to bits just because you're out of action. Judy and Helen can manage that later.'

'You don't understand——' But he was leading her out of the kitchen, supporting her so firmly that it was almost as if he were carrying her, and she didn't have to put her weight on her left foot at all.

'Right. Feet up, that's it. Want the fire lighting?'

'N-no, thanks.' One last sniff, and the tears had nearly gone.

'A few magazines? I've got some very interesting ones in my room.'

She hesitated. Why not? 'Yes, please.' He went out quietly, and Jan was left alone. She lay back with her head on a cushion and closed her eyes. What's the matter with me? she thought. I must be mad. She was asleep within minutes, and never heard Breck return.

There was no doubt about who was in charge now. It was Saturday lunchtime, and Jan was in the living room, her feet up, a blanket over her knees, and a good fire going in the fireplace. Magazines were on the carpet well within reach, and Helen popped her head round the door. 'Breck says do you need anything before he goes to meet the ferry?'

'Tell him nothing, thanks.' She picked up one of his magazines after Helen had vanished, but she saw nothing of the print. Her mind went over all that had happened in the previous twenty-four hours. One day, and the situation had changed so drastically that she would not have believed it possible. But it was . . .

She had woken up because she was hungry that Friday afternoon. The Hoover whirred away in the distance, but that was the only sound. Jan had struggled to her feet and attempted to walk to the door. It was impossible. Just a few steps told her that, and she sank back on the settee with a grimace of pain.

There was a slight movement outside the door, and Judy's head appeared—then the rest of her as she saw Jan sitting up. 'Oh, you're awake. He told me to look again—he's a bossy pig!'

'I'm starving. Is there anything left?'

'Yes. We left some curry on a low light. You know something? It wasn't too awful!' and she vanished.

Jan had eaten the hot spicy curry, and had enjoyed it. It was quiet—too quiet. She longed to be up and about, and knowing what was going on. She was not used to this inactivity and it was so irksome that when Breck had eventually come in, she said: 'I can't just sit here all day.'

'What do you suggest? Helen's getting the bedroom ready, Judy's doing our dinner, and your father is still in his den. And I'm just going to finish the windows. You'd like to hold the ladder perhaps?'

'No! But—oh, you don't understand!'

'I do, but you'll just have to be patient. Everything's going smoothly. The washer's going at full speed. There's nothing you can do without getting hopelessly in the way.'

'Thanks,' she answered in a very dry tone.

'Don't mention it. If you want me, shout out.' He turned to go out, paused, and added: 'And don't try and walk on your own, or you'll be even longer.'

Jan put down the magazine with a sigh. The rest of Friday had passed very slowly, as had this morning. And in an hour or so, someone called Terry would arrive. Another alien, like Breck himself. Breck—who had already managed to take over most effectively. He had threatened to tame Jan. He could hardly have foreseen her falling from a ladder—but he had taken the utmost advantage from it. While she was helpless he had subtly assumed command. Why? That was something she didn't understand. Most men would shy away from anything not involved directly with their own sphere of activity, would have left the work to Judy and Helen—and kept out of the way. She lay back, too puzzled and disturbed to read any of the magazines he had lent her. They were glossies, very expensive, several American and some in French and German, and covering a variety of subjects. But one thing they all had in common were articles concerning television. Brainwashing! thought Jan in disgust, but she had read one on a TV expedition to a remote village in Patagonia that had resulted in a new wonder drug being discovered, made from the leaves of a certain plant that the villagers had used for centuries. Several hospital patients in Britain and other countries were now responding to treatment with the drug. And all as a result of a camera and team going on a long journey...

'Oh! I'm fed up!' she spoke aloud.

'Are you? You must be feeling much better.' She jumped at the sound of Breck's voice from the doorway.

'I thought you'd gone to meet the ferry,' she said, confused.

'Just going. Are you sure you don't want anything?'

'Nothing at all. I could walk with a stick, you know.'

'Could you? We'll try when I get back. Until then, be patient.'

'All right.' She smiled, because she had no intention of doing so. The idea had only just come to her, and she could not wait to try it. 'Goodbye.'

'Au revoir.' He went then, with a mocking salute, and she was alone again. She listened hard until she heard the sound of his Land-Rover starting up, then the sound diminished as he went down the drive. Now was the moment. Jan stood up and hopped to the door, pausing for breath before she shouted out: 'Judy—Helen?'

An answering call, then Helen appeared, wiping her hands on a towel. 'What do you want—what are you doing there?'

'I hopped!' Jan answered mischievously. 'I'm going to try and walk with a stick. Will you get me those two by the back door?'

'That's funny,' Helen answered. 'I was only

86

thinking of them—but Breck's just taken them with him in the Land-Rover. How strange. I wonder what he wants them for?'

'I think I can tell you,' answered Jan grimly. 'But I won't.' The arrogance of the man. The sheer *arrogance*! 'I'll wait until he gets back.' She hopped painfully back to her seat, seething with resentment. He didn't trust her. She was too annoyed to realize that it was with justification.

Nearly an hour had passed, and they waited for the men to arrive, and Jan sipped hot tea and wondered if Terry could possibly be as bad as Breck. No, that would be impossible. But he was still an intruder—a man from television, and therefore equally not to be trusted...

'I can hear the Land-Rover,' said Judy, and went to the window. 'Yes, it's him, and—oh!' she stopped.

'What?' asked Jan, frustrated at not being able to move. 'What's the matter?'

'Well, there's a very tall thin creature unfolding itself from the passenger seat—ugh! It's got a beard—and the weirdest clothes.'

Jan sat back. In a moment they'd come in, and she would see for herself.

'It's not so bad as that,' remarked Helen thoughtfully. 'It looks almost human to me.' They might, to anyone overhearing them, have been discussing a new species of insect they had discovered, thought Jan. 'Look, Judy, it's laughing.'

'Hmm!' Judy said severely. 'Probably because Breck's told it we're all quite nutty here.'

'Mind out,' Helen dived towards the settee. 'They're coming in.'

Silence. It was possible to hear the faint footsteps growing louder. Then there came a knock at the door.

'Come in,' Jan called. And the horrible picture she had conjured up in her mind shattered into a thousand tiny fragments as the two men walked in. They were both of an identical height, but there the resemblance ended. Terry was painfully thin, and it was true that a black beard covered a portion of his face, but what she could see Jan instantly liked—despite all her mind told her. For this was a man who looked as if he not only found life a lot of fun—but that he couldn't help sharing that fun with others. The broad smile was genuine, the laughing brown eyes were looking straight at her, and he walked across the room and said in a pleasant voice as he took her hand: 'I'm sorry to hear about your accident. I'm Terry Smith, it's very good of you to put me up. I hope you'll accept a few chocolates—they might make you feel slightly better.' His left hand had been behind his back. He produced a small box and handed it to her with a flourish. Liqueurs, Jan's favourite. From the corner of her eye she saw Helen go faintly pink, and knew that someone had been asking questions. She would really have to have a talk with that child . . .

'Thank you very much. My sisters, Judy and Helen.'

'Hello,' he took their hands, and a strange thing happened when he shook Judy's. Jan saw embarrassment in her eyes, a faint pinkness to her cheeks as she said: 'Hello,' in return. Not Judy! Helen, yes, but Judy was quite immune to men.

When they had gone out again to take Terry's

88

cases upstairs, Jan said: 'Judy? What on *earth's* the matter with you?'

Judy looked at her. 'Nothing. Why?' The pinkness had vanished now.

Jan shrugged. 'I don't know. You seemed—different, somehow.'

'Well, he was different from what I'd expected—not like *him*, I mean. He's not—not bad really. He looks as if he's always laughing—oh! what's the use—what silly questions!' and she dashed out and slammed the door behind her.

Helen looked across at Jan and smiled faintly. 'I do believe our Judy is smitten!'

'Mmm, she is acting very strangely. And anyway, how, I would like to know, did young Terry guess the right chocolates for me?'

'Oh,' Helen said. 'Well, Breck sort of asked me, you see, before he went.'

'Yes, I thought so. You two seem very pally.'

Helen immediately assumed a lofty disdain. 'Pally? Really, Jan, that's *ridiculous*! I can hardly go round snubbing him when he asks perfectly harmless questions, can I? I'm going to see what Judy's doing.' And she began to walk to the door with great dignity. 'I'll bring you a cup of coffee,' she said kindly, as she reached it. 'You look as though you need something.'

The door closed. Jan was alone again. She tore the cellophane from the box of chocolates and opened it. Perhaps there would be slight consolation in a nice gooey liqueur. Because for some absurd reason she felt quite as though she had been abandoned by all her nearest and dearest. First Judy, then Helen. And no doubt two men laughing upstairs over the crazy household they had landed themselves in. 'I don't *care*,' she told herself as she bit firmly into a luscious-looking chocolate that had born the words 'Cognac' on its golden wrapper. But it was not true. She did care.

CHAPTER SIX

THERE was no doubt about it. Terry was completely different from Breck in so many ways. He was like a breath of invigorating fresh air would be to someone who had been shut away in a stuffy room. Jan sat in the kitchen later that afternoon and watched him at work. She was, she told herself, merely there to see how true Breck's words were about his culinary skills. She had pushed firmly to the back of her mind the reason why he was there at all. Later, she would think about it. Not now. Breck had vanished in the Land-Rover. A huge box of groceries that Terry had brought from the mainland still waited to be unpacked, and Jan, although dying of curiosity, would not permit herself to ask what was in it.

The subject of television, and documentaries, had not been mentioned at all. Not once. Instead Terry and Jan talked about their favourite recipes, sport, problems of accommodation in London. He was funny and he was very intelligent, and she wondered what her attitude would have been if he had come first to the island, and not Breck. But strangely, at the thought of Breck, her heart gave a lurch, and she wondered where he had gone...

'What about goulash?'

'What?' she had been miles away.

'Ever tried your hand at a Hungarian goulash?'

'No. Well, not recently. I do the odd curry—why do you ask?' She was intrigued.

He nodded towards the cardboard box. 'I'll unload that in a moment. I had a pleasant hour's shopping before I caught the ferry. It's dead simple to make. Fancy one tonight?'

'Yes.'

'Good. Breck told me you're a super cook. I shall have to be on my mettle, won't I?' So Breck had actually praised her! She was almost too surprised to speak for a moment.

'Heavens! I'm not—I just enjoy cooking, that's all.' But she wondered fleetingly if Breck had also mentioned the cold porridge, and other things...

'And I bought some things to make Chinese meals as well. I think I'm going to enjoy being here, Jan. I'll be honest, I wasn't looking forward to it at all.'

'Oh! You weren't?'

He laughed. 'Don't sound so dismayed! A job's a job, and we take what comes, and Breck's the best boss anyone could have, but he does tend to bulldoze everyone round to his way of thinking——' he stopped.

Jan smiled. 'That I can imagine!'

'No, don't get me wrong. That just slipped out. He has the ability to get the best out of everybody. I'm damned glad I'm his P.A.'

'P.A.? What does that mean?'

'Sorry. Production assistant, actually. I'm the one who's supposed to go round the place knocking on doors and charming everyone into allowing us into their homes to talk and generally give us their opinions of life here.'

Jan fiddled with an empty beaker before her on the table. 'I suppose,' she said hesitantly, 'he's told you what our thoughts are on that matter?'

He grinned. 'Yes. Hey, let me pour you some more coffee. Can I have some too?'

'Of course.' She handed him the beaker.

'I'm sorry about that, Jan. I'm the last one to want to intrude on anyone's life—and I appreciate your viewpoint, although I'll bet you don't believe me. But you know Breck—well, perhaps you don't, not very well anyway—once he gets the bit in his teeth it's all go, plus the fact of his grandparents coming from——' he stopped, and Jan saw the dawning look of dismay on his face.

'What? What's the matter?' she even looked quickly round in case some dread apparition had appeared in the doorway behind her. There was nobody there. 'Coming from *where*?' she asked.

Terry groaned, handing her the beaker. 'He'll kill me.'

'He won't get the chance if you don't finish that sentence!' Her eyes gleamed.

'Can't you guess? Please don't let him know I told you. For some reason he doesn't want it known, goodness knows why. His grandparents came from here. This island.'

She couldn't really take it in. 'But it was only through my sister Diane——' she began.

'No, not exactly.' He pulled up a chair and sat beside her. 'I've gone too far now. I'll tell you the full story. Breck knows Diane's husband, Jack, well. I was with him at one of those ghastly parties given for some visiting foreign television bigwigs when we met Diane. He expressed interest in Diane's accent, so she told him where she came from—and after that the sole topic of conversation was the Dark Isle. He seemed absolutely fascinated in finding everything out about it that he could.'

Jan digested this amazing information in silence. How strange that Breck hadn't mentioned the fact once. 'You won't say a word, will you?' Terry looked quite worried. Solemnly Jan crossed her heart.

'I give you my word,' she said.

He grinned, back to normal again. 'Okay. Now, let's see what we have in our box of goodies, shall we?' He lifted the box on to the table in front of her. She had the feeling of anticipation she had had as a child, on birthdays, and the next quarter hour or so was spent in surveying what Terry had called 'goodies'.

He must have spent pounds on them. She looked at him in dismay as he produced a long blue packet of spaghetti, and said: 'The money—I'm afraid——'

He laughed. 'On the house—or rather on our beloved TV company—don't worry about a thing, Jan, honest.'

She looked at the colourful array of tins and packages set out before her. 'It's not right,' she said.

'What isn't? Eating?'

'No, all this——' she pointed vaguely. 'I can't explain it. I tried to, to Breck, but he's about as understanding as that wall over there.'

'Is he?' Terry gave her a shrewd look, and although he still smiled, there was a serious air to him now. 'I think you may find that Breck understands a lot more than he appears to.' He paused. 'He told me what you'd said before—when you had your accident.'

'He did?' She shouldn't have been surprised, she knew.

'About the money?'

'Yes.'

'Oh!' She felt her lips tighten helplessly. Why it should so disturb her, she could not understand—but it did. She moved uneasily on her chair, and felt for the two walking sticks with which she could manage to move about—albeit very slowly. 'I must go and just——' she began.

'Don't—don't go, Jan. I'm sorry. Have I upset you?'

'No.' She swallowed hard. How did you begin to explain to anyone that a man like Breck could have such an effect on you—when you didn't even understand yourself? 'No. I'll be back in a few minutes.'

'Then we'll start the goulash. Right?'

'Right.' She made her slow way to the door, and was nearly knocked flying by Judy dashing in.

'Whoops! Sorry, Jan.' But Judy's eyes were already on Terry. Judy the man-hater, who seemed to have changed in the past few hours into a blushing teenager. 'It's Daddy. He wants to meet Terry.'

That was quite surprising in itself. Jan looked at him. He was already taking off the tea-towel he had been using as a pinafore tucked into his rather vivid orange jeans.

'Right. Where—er—is he?'

'In his den. Come on, I'll show you. I think Breck must have told him you liked *making* things,' Judy announced wide-eyed.

'Oh, I see.' Was he actually going a bit red? Jan wondered.

'Don't tell me you're one as well?' she said.

'Er—well, not an inventor actually, but yes, I do dabble a bit. I've had one or two things patented. They don't make much money, but——' he shrugged. 'You know how it is. I wanted to meet him very much.'

Jan stood by the door. 'I don't see how you'll ever get any work done while you're here,' she told him. 'I mean if you're going to be cooking all the time, and now talking to Daddy—I warn you, you'll never get away once he starts. You'll have to be *firm*—tell him you've got the dinner to do. And if he asks why, it'll only be because he's forgotten I've hurt my ankle, so you'll have to remind him.'

Terry laughed. 'You mean he gets absorbed with his work to the exclusion of everything else?'

'I mean he doesn't always know what *day* it is, once he locks himself away. You may do him good, Terry. Go on now. I'll wait here for you.'

She watched them go. Life was full of surprises. First the news of Breck's ancestry, and now Terry. What, she wondered, would be next?

She had hidden the exercise book in a kitchen cupboard where nobody but she went. It seemed an ideal opportunity. Terry had been gone over fifteen minutes—and she knew he would be at least another half hour. Judy would be with them. Helen had gone to visit old Mrs. MacPhail, and would be ages. And Breck—where was he? She didn't know, but she would hear the Land-Rover in good time.

Jan lifted out the tattered book and her two pens, and put them on the kitchen table. Not even her sisters knew about it. No one did. She would put it aside for days at a time, but always it was there, in the back of her mind—the pictures, the people, the events, forming a huge jigsaw that only she could piece together into the pages of that beloved exercise book. All her life, for as long as she could remember, and since the days when she had first been able to hold a pen in chubby fingers, Jan had written. At first it had been little rhymes, then short stories which she had read to her sisters at bedtime, and then articles about life on the island. They were all locked away in an old box in her bedroom. But even then, all those years ago, the burning desire to write a novel had been forming at the back of her mind. And six months previously, because at last the idea would no longer be contained in her head, Jan had started it. Two exercise books were already filled and hidden away with the older, childish stories in her room. A historical adventure, set in the early nineteenth century; Jan could become so absorbed sometimes that she was unaware of anything except the rich tapestry that unfolded itself on to paper before her.

And it was so now. Once she began, and her busy hand raced over the thin lined paper, Jan became totally immersed in her writing. She didn't know if what she was putting down was good yet. There was a deep satisfaction to the task, a certain pleasure in seeing the words formed on the paper. And if possible, it was only enhanced by the knowledge that no one save her knew anything about it.

Leonora was hiding in her grandfather's cottage in the forest. Lord Aragon was searching for her, but he would not find her there, for he didn't know of her relationship to the old man. Leonora hated Lord Aragon with all her young heart, and one day she would be avenged for the murder of her younger brother, Peter, who had been working on the grand Aragon estates at the time he met his death...

She was not alone. It took a minute or two for the realization to penetrate Jan's brain, so absorbed had she been in describing Leonora's feelings as she stood hiding behind the curtain, watching for the man— She turned round, wild-eyed, cheeks flushed, one hand going instinctively to cover the page of writing. And saw Breck Fallon right behind her, so close that he must have seen...

'I'm sorry if I frightened you,' the voice was mocking, soft. 'But you were so engrossed in your writing I feared to disturb you.' His eyes were on the book. Jan closed it. He sat down at the table, at an angle to her. 'Are you writing a story?'

'Did you see anything?' she hated to ask, but she had to. She *must* know.

'Yes.'

'W-what did you see?'

'Do you want the exact words? I saw: "Leonora's fingers tightened on the coarse material that hung at the window. In a minute Lord Aragon would appear. Oh, if she were only a man——" That's all—that's as far as you got.'

'You are despicable,' she said softly.

'Why? Because you didn't hear me come in? Should I have knocked? I didn't know you'd be alone. I thought Terry was doing the dinner in here, if you must know. There are more private places for writing, come to that.'

She stared at him, helpless because he had an answer for everything, vulnerable because now he knew her secret—and how he must be laughing! If he smiled—even slightly—she would hit him, she knew.

But he wasn't smiling, not even fractionally. He seemed quite serious as he went on: 'If you are writing, and you don't want anyone to know about it, that's entirely your own affair. Presumably I'm "despicable" because you immediately assumed I'd burst into loud guffaws of laughter and rush around telling everyone—oh, it's all right, I can tell by your face that you did. The trouble with you is you're so damned prickly and suspicious about everyone—or is it just me that has this effect on you?'

'How did you guess?' her eyes sparkled with suppressed anger.

'Ah, so that's it. Well, well, now I know, don't I?' And then he laughed. 'At least you're honest. And what a temper you've got! I'm surprised your hair's not a flaming shade of red! I've already told you it won't get you anywhere with me—although I'm sure you'll put the fear of God into poor Terry if you choose to——'

'I wouldn't want to! *He's* nice.'

'Is he now? I'm relieved to know you think so. There'll be no crockery flying around the kitchen at least, for which we'll all be thankful——'

'Go away,' she whispered, trembling.

'Not until I'm ready. You're hardly in a position to order me around, in your delicate condition.'

'Then I'll go. I'm not staying here listening to you.' She stood up with difficulty, and picked up a walking stick. She looked at the exercise book. She couldn't leave *that* there. And she wouldn't ask him to pass it to her either. So she leaned over the table and tried to pick it up—and in doing so, overbalanced. He was up, and caught her, to steady her, in a split second. Humiliating enough itself,

99

but his laughter added to it and she struggled furiously to shake him off.

'Let *go* of me!'

'Hold it, little tiger. Do you want to go sprawling? You will if you keep fighting like that.'

'I *hate* you laughing.' She glared furiously at him, dark hair tumbling about her face.

'It's either that or crying. You'd drive any man to distraction. You are the most infuriating woman——'

'I thought I was a kid to you?' she snapped.

'Ah, so that still rankles, does it? Hmm, interesting. I must remember.' And he released her slowly, still grinning. It was the grin that did it. Mocking, too knowing. With her free hand she struck out at him, but he caught her hand in mid-air and held her wrist in a grip of steel. 'Now, just remember what I told you,' his grey eyes gleamed, hard and cool. 'Don't think your ankle will let you get away with it. Nobody hits me.'

'If I were a man I would. I hate you,' she breathed. 'Let me go at once!'

'But you're not. So try and remember that fact. And certainly I'll let you go—as long as you're sure you can stand up.' And he did so.

Jan turned and walked slowly, painfully, *seething*, out of the kitchen. It wasn't until she reached the living room that she realized she had left her exercise book behind. She stood in the doorway for a moment as a wave of alarm swept her. She must go back right now. The walk had made her foot throb, and going back was distressing and more slow, but the urge to get there was stronger than any pain, and she made it at last, and pushed the door open.

Breck Fallon was standing there and he was

reading what she had written. He didn't even have the grace to look guilty at being caught red-handed, merely looked from it to her and said: 'I thought you'd be back when you remembered. I was just about to fetch it in to you.'

'It looks like it,' she retorted furiously.

'Oh, I was—cross my heart. I'm a very fast reader, and your writing's clear. I'd nearly finished, actually.' He closed it and walked towards her. 'Aren't you going to ask me how I like it?'

'No!'

'Pity.' He handed it to her. 'There you are, then. Oh, you'll want your pens, won't you?' He went back to the table.

'How *dare* you read what I've written without my permission!' She nearly snatched the pens from him.

Breck raised a questioning eyebrow. 'Why? It's not a letter. It's a book—you'll expect a publisher to read it eventually.'

'I won't. What a stupid thing to say!'

'Stupid? How else will you get it published?'

'I'm writing it because I want to, that's all. I'm not interested in anyone else seeing what I've written.'

'Then you are the stupid one, not me. I shouldn't imagine there's much satisfaction in slaving away to write a book if you're then going to put it in a drawer and forget it—still, I wouldn't pretend to understand your mind, it's obviously completely different from mine.'

'Obviously.' She was getting tired standing there. Her leg ached now, and her arm was still sore enough to remind her of its graze. 'Can I go now?' She was not aware that she had gone pale, yet she saw something reflected briefly in Breck's eyes, and he said softly:

'I'd sit down if I were you, before you fall.'

'I'm all right——' but she swayed slightly as she said it.

'No, you're not. Sit down now——' then as she held tightly to her precious book: 'It's all right, I'm not trying to take it from you.' His hand on her arm guided her to the chair. 'All right now? Want a drink?'

Her good elbow was on the table, and she leaned forward and put her hand to her forehead. 'I think so. Anything.'

'Tea it will be.'

She watched him put the kettle on and rinse out the teapot. It had happened again; an abrupt change of mood from the brittle aggression of their conflict to concern. And there was something she had to ask. She could not help herself. 'Why did you say what you did about a publisher?'

'Forget it. It's nothing to do with me.' He spoke completely casually. 'And you're in no state to argue. You don't have sugar in your tea, do you?'

'No, thanks. Please,' she said softly.

He turned slowly. 'Please? From you? There's a change. All right, I'll tell you. If I said it's the best thing I'd ever read you'd not believe a word of it. But how would you react if I said that your writing is quite good?'

She shrugged helplessly. 'I don't know. Is it?'

'It's promising. You have a nice way of expressing yourself—on paper.'

She didn't miss the significance of that slight pause before the last two words, but she was too interested in what he was saying to bother about it.

No one had ever commented on her writing before, except her two sisters, and they enjoyed every word, as children, but this was vastly different.

'And you think I should send it to a publisher?'

'When it's finished, and typed out—yes. I wanted to go on reading, and that's the best test of *any* writing. It can be technically perfect, but if it doesn't hold your interest then the author has failed.'

Jan bit her lip. She could hardly believe what she was hearing. 'I'll remember what you said,' she answered eventually.

'Do.' It was almost as if he had lost interest. As he poured out tea, handed her the beaker, the subject of writing might never have been brought up. Perversely, it was annoying to Jan—but it was entirely her own fault, she knew that. She drank her tea, and then Terry reappeared, and everything became normal again—for a while. The two men got on well together, you could tell, and as usual, when anyone else was present, Breck's manner with Jan was politely casual, the brittle tension hidden—but there, even so.

They began to prepare dinner, only now it was three of them, then Judy and Helen came in and showed great interest in the array of foodstuffs that Terry had bought, and Jan thought: It only needs Daddy to appear and it'll be a party.

She couldn't keep her writing in the kitchen any longer. When she went up to her bedroom after a while she hid it in the box with the others. She was confused and uncertain about Breck's words. But she still didn't know why.

On Sunday the island was mist-shrouded and silent; a different place. Terry stood at the kitchen window and looked out, utterly fascinated.

'Incredible,' he said. 'What atmosphere! I've never seen anything like it!'

Jan began laughing. 'We get them all the time,' she told him. 'Either that or rain—take your pick.'

'Super. I'm beginning to see this place in a new light altogether. I never thought I would.'

'What do you mean?'

'I can see the fascination it must hold for you and your family.'

'Except Diane,' Jan said dryly.

'Mmm—I know what you mean. But she painted such a vivid picture to Breck and me that he couldn't wait to get here, don't forget.'

'He had other reasons,' she reminded him.

'I know, but apart from that even. He——' he broke off as the door opened, and Breck came in. 'Ah, there you are. I was just telling Jan what a fantastic atmosphere they have here.'

'I've just been out to check the Land-Rover,' said Breck. 'It nearly drowned me!' He ran his fingers through his wet hair. 'It's like breathing through wet cottonwool.'

'That's it!' Terry clicked his fingers. 'I must go out for a quick walk—soak up the atmosphere.'

'You'll do that all right—literally,' Breck told him. 'Rather you than me. And don't fall and break a leg. There's a limit to the number of P.A.s they'll send out here, you know.'

'See you.' With a careless wave, Terry left them. There was silence for a few moments, then Breck spoke.

'He's mad,' he announced. 'Quite nuts.' He looked at Jan. 'And how are you today?'

'Much better, thank you.' But her voice felt stilted. She wondered why she could never relax with him. There was always the tension when they were alone. Try as she might, she could not dispel it. 'You were right about Terry.'

'Oh, in what way?'

'About his cooking, I mean. He really is superb.'

'The goulash was quite something. But you helped, didn't you?'

'Yes. But he told me what to do, I just listened.'

'Mm—*that's* a change,' he said very dryly. 'Mind if I make myself a coffee?'

'Feel free. And do you think you're funny?'

He laughed. 'No. Did my remark upset you?'

'Not at all,' she answered, as if surprised. 'But sarcasm is the lowest form of wit.'

'I seem to have heard that before somewhere,' he grinned at her from the sink, where he was filling a kettle. 'Couldn't you be more original?'

'If I made the effort—but it's hardly worth it, with you,' she answered sweetly.

'Ouch!' he grimaced as if in pain. 'That's better! More of the old Jan. Getting the fire back, are we? You must be feeling better.'

He lit the gas and put the kettle on. 'We start work tomorrow. Going round the islanders, I mean. Sounding out their reactions about being interviewed in their homes.'

'They know all about you already,' she answered. 'You don't think any newcomer can be here for more than five minutes without having everything known about him, do you?' And she watched to see what his reaction would be. Would he tell her about his grandparents? She could not mention it; she was bound by a promise. But if he did, that

105

would be different...

'Really? Different from London. No one gives a damn there. Still, I suppose you're used to it.'

'Yes. It works both ways.'

'I don't follow you.'

'I mean, if anyone's ill, they don't go without help. I've read in papers about people living alone who are taken ill—and no one knows, or cares. That couldn't happen here. There's a very old lady, Mrs. MacPhail, who's ill. Helen went to see her yesterday and took her some fresh vegetables and meat and eggs. Another neighbour does her housework for her while she's poorly. I may go to-morrow——' she stopped, remembering. 'Oh! I can't—I'd forgotten about my foot. Judy can go.'

'No, I'll take you.' He rinsed two beakers. 'What you've just said is very interesting. Just the kind of thing we need in this programme. The human touch, the way everyone cares—yes, I like that.' She wondered if he was being sarcastic, but only for a moment. His face was thoughtful. And suddenly she realized something. Mrs. MacPhail was over ninety, and had lived on the island all her life. She would have known Breck's grandparents. She knew everyone.

'If she gets better, she'd be ideal to interview,' Jan said casually, watching for any reaction. 'She knows everything there is to know about this place. she's ninety-two—or three, I'm not sure which, and she'll talk for hours if you let her—or at least, she will when she's well.'

'What's the matter with her?'

'She fell and broke her leg a couple of months ago. They took her by helicopter to the mainland for hospital treatment. We all thought that she wouldn't get better—but she's very strong—and it's rumoured she made life very difficult for the hospital staff——' Jan couldn't help a little smile as she said the words. She knew the old woman too well—'so they had to let her come home. She gets around with a stick now, and still manages all her work, but she's had a bad cold, so we persuaded her to take it easy—and *that's* not easy, I can tell you—so we have a sort of rota now.'

'Fascinating!' He was beginning to sound like Terry. 'I must meet her. Can't we go today?'

'On *Sunday!* She won't see you on the Sabbath!' Jan laughed. 'She'd be horrified. She may not even talk to *you* tomorrow. She doesn't believe in television either. So don't say I didn't warn you.'

He nodded. 'We'll see. Helicopter, eh? That's something I hadn't thought about.' He produced a small notebook from the pocket of his denim jacket, and began writing. Then he looked up. 'Anyone else I should see?'

'Quite a few. But I thought that was Terry's job?' she answered.

'Mmm, yes. But there are no rules about it. Will you let me take you to this old lady's house tomorrow?'

It was a change, she thought, for him to be asking her something—and in quite a pleasant manner. 'If you wish,' she said. 'As long as you promise not to'—she hesitated—'well, she's very old—I don't want her upset in any way.'

Breck gave her a long cool look. 'You were going to tell me not to bully her, weren't you? What do you think I am? No, don't answer that.' He suddenly laughed. 'You may be surprised when you see me in action.'

'Oh, I'm sure I will,' Jan murmured. Their eyes met in a sudden challenge—and it was Jan who looked away first. It was happening again, this prickly unease with him. I wish you'd never come, she thought, watching him as he poured their coffee out a few minutes later. But deep down inside, she knew it wasn't strictly true.

CHAPTER SEVEN

'TELL me which way now,' Breck told Jan as he drove the Land-Rover along a narrow road which branched a few hundred yards ahead. They were in a thickly wooded part of the island, and tall trees met overhead in a green canopy that hid the sun from them.

'To the right,' Jan said. 'You'll see several houses. Mrs. McPhail's is the first one.'

He drove on, took the fork as she had directed, and stopped in front of the row of small cottages. They had left the trees behind them now, and the sun shone brilliantly down, gleaming on the water of the loch that lay to their right. On the other side of the loch were mountains, blue and grey in that morning light, cool and remote.

Breck stood for a few minutes at the side of his Land-Rover, just looking out over the water, and Jan was able to study him unobserved. His gaze was encompassing, taking it all in, the deep intelligent look of a man who knew precisely what he was doing, where he was going in life. Tall, broad-shouldered, apparently quite unselfconscious, he stood there, and something Terry had said came back to Jan. 'He has women after him,' he had told her. 'And he enjoys their company, but I can't see him ever settling down to marriage—the woman who could hold him hasn't been invented yet.' She could believe that to be true. She turned away suddenly, unable to stand still any longer.

'I'll knock and see if she's up,' she told him, keeping her voice very casual. 'I'll not be a minute.'

He didn't turn round. 'Shout me when you're ready,' he answered.

The door was never locked. After tapping, Jan opened it and went into the tiny hallway that always smelt of polish and lavender, a scent that immediately brought back pleasant childhood memories.

'Mrs. MacPhail, it's me, Jan,' she called loudly.

'Come away in, child, I'm in the front parlour.' The voice was high and clear. The old lady was sitting by the fire, a tartan rug over her knees, knitting on her lap, which she put down at Jan's entrance.

'There you are,' she sniffed. 'I was wondering how long it would take you to come in. I've been watching you. Is that *him*?'

Jan laughed and went over to kiss the old woman. 'Yes. So you've been spying, have you? He wants to see you.'

'Aye well, tell him to come in, then. I'm quite respectable. I had the feeling you'd be here today, so I got up early.'

Jan looked at the calm, very wrinkled face that was turned towards her, the clear pale eyes of Mrs. MacPhail that missed nothing. The old woman's white hair was pulled back and tied with a blue ribbon. She looked very fragile and very old.

'I'll bring him in, then.' She went to open the door. 'You can come in, Breck,' she called. Movement was slow, because she was still clumsy with the stick, but she held the door for him. He had to duck his head in the low doorway, and he went forward with his hand outstretched to greet the old woman who sat like a queen waiting to receive him.

'Breck Fallon,' Jan murmured. 'He's from London.'

'Aye, I know.' Shrewd pale eyes took in the length of him in a quick assessment. 'Sit you down, young man, you're too big to stand. Pull up that chair and let me look at you.'

Jan hid a smile. The encounter might be interesting. She sat in a highbacked chair by the window and watched Breck obediently pull up a chair for himself.

Mrs. MacPhail nodded. 'That's it. I can see you better now. Can you wind wool?'

'I've never tried,' he confessed.

'Then it's time you learned. I don't believe in wasting time. You can wind it while we talk. So you're from the television, are you? And what are you going to do to our beautiful little island, eh?' She pulled a skein of bright yellow wool from a knitting bag beside her and handed it to him. 'Arms apart—no, that's not wide enough. That'll do. See, I will take this end, and you must move your hands so, and I will make a ball of wool.' She spoke patiently, as if to a child, and Jan, who was biting back laughter, could stand it no longer.

'I'll put the kettle on for tea,' she managed to say, and made her way as fast as she could to the kitchen. Safely there she put her hand to her mouth to stifle the giggles that threatened to escape. If Breck Fallon had imagined he would be talking to a simple old dear, he was having to adjust rapidly. She heard his voice in reply, his deep tones which were in such contrast to Mrs. MacPhail's, and she heard him explaining what they intended doing. She filled the kettle and looked in the cupboard for cups and saucers. Only half listening now, she was suddenly startled into awareness as she heard the old woman say:

'Have you Scots blood in you?' Jan paused and put down three saucers very quietly. And waited for him to answer.

'Yes. What made you ask?'

'Ach! I can tell. You're no Sassenach. It's there in that proud look of you—and in your eyes. Where are you from?'

'My grandparents were Scots. My mother's parents, I mean.' There was a pause, and Jan heard Mrs. MacPhail's voice quite clearly:

'And I do not think it was so far away from here. Am I correct?'

'You are. How did you know, Mrs. MacPhail?'

'Didn't Jan tell you? I have the gift—the second sight. I see more than I can tell. Give me your hand again.' Jan, despite herself, felt a tiny shiver run down her spine. There was something eerie about the old woman's ability to sum up people in minutes. She stood very still, and as the kettle began to shrill, moved it quickly from the heat, so that she could listen.

'Ach yes. You have an honest hand—like your face. I would not have you in my house if I did not like you. Were they from this island?'

'Yes, they were.'

'And the name? Tell me their name.'

'MacLeod.'

'Ah, yes. I knew—I *knew*. See, pass me that old box from under the table. I will show you something.'

Jan put the kettle back on again, and brewed the tea, went for the milk from the stone floor of the pantry, and poured it into the cups. Her hand shook slightly. She had not imagined anything like this happening. She wanted very much to see Breck's face.

When she carried the first cup and saucer in, Breck stood up. 'I'll bring the others in,' he said. 'Sit down, Jan.' There was a box of old photographs on the old woman's knee, and she was going through them with slow fingers. Jan went to her chair and sat down. In a way, she was no part of this. Breck looked like a man who had had a shock; she felt almost sorry for him. But she didn't know why she should be. He had wanted to come, had asked to be brought here. And yet ... She didn't know what it was. Terry had said that Breck didn't want it known about his grandparents. Perhaps he was surprised, that was all.

'There you are.' She had found something, was handing a photograph to him. Jan watched his face as he looked at it. She couldn't see what it was of from where she sat, but she saw his face tighten, the dark set to his mouth.

'Those are your grandparents. Do you not know where they lived?'

'No.' He said the word very quietly.

'It was just a few doors away. I knew—there was something when you walked in—I think I knew who you were.'

He looked at her. 'Did you? I believe you did. Does anyone live in their house at present?'

'No. It is empty. Jan, the house where old Mrs. MacLeod lived—take Breck along to see it. Do you want to go there?' she asked him.

'Yes. I think I'd like to—after I've drunk this.'

The old woman sat back and chuckled. 'I'm never mistaken,' she said. 'And when you've had a look, you come back here. I'll tell you all you want to know about this place for your television programme. Is your mother still living?'

'Yes. She's a doctor. So is my father.'

'Aye, that I can imagine. Your grandfather was very good with herbs and plants. Everyone went to him when they were ill——'

Jan went quietly out to the kitchen with her empty cup. She felt like an intruder. Their conversation was nothing to do with her. She stayed there, having closed the door to the living room, leaving the two of them to talk in private while she prepared the old lady's lunch and put it to simmer slowly on the gas. She heard her name called and went in.

'Away you go now. Come back when you've seen the wee house,' Mrs. MacPhail told them, and watched them go.

Jan pushed open the door of the empty cottage and went in followed by Breck. He stood there looking round the tiny room with faded wallpaper, and soot in the black fireplace, and a mark on the wall where a picture had hung.

'So this is it,' he said softly.

'Did you come to Dark Isle hoping to find this place?' Jan asked.

He looked at her. 'Yes, I did. You heard us talking?'

'Of course.' He walked away from her, into the tiny kitchen that was covered in a fine film of dust. She was seeing a different aspect of the man—yet again. 'But then—when Mrs. MacPhail began tell-

ing you about your grandfather's skill with herbs—
I closed the door.'

'I know you did. Why?'

'It was nothing to do with me,' she said simply.

Breck looked at her. 'Wasn't it? I'm having my
eyes opened today, in more ways than one.' The
words seemed to have some significance that she
didn't understand, yet, strangely, she didn't want
to ask him. He went over to the window, and
looked out at the tangled bushes growing wild outside. 'So this is the place,' he said softly. 'I've seen it
at last—I didn't imagine I would, somehow.'

'Have a look upstairs,' Jan said. 'Take as long as
you like. I'll go back to Mrs. MacPhail and check
that the meal I put on is all right.'

'Did you know my grandparents?'

'Yes.' She paused on her way to the front door. 'I
was only a child when they died, but I remember
your grandfather well. He once fished me out of
the loch when I was only four. I think he saved my
life.'

She went out, because if she stayed there a moment longer, she knew she would start to cry. Mrs.
MacPhail knew. She knew everything.

'You left him there?' she asked sharply.

'Yes.' Jan sat down. 'I think he wanted to be
alone. I told him that his grandfather had fished
me out of the water. Then I left him.'

'He is bitter about them. Do you know why?'

'No, he hasn't told me. It's none of my business.'

'I wonder?' the old woman asked softly, and
smiled. 'It may be.'

Jan had had enough of cryptic remarks for one
day. 'I'll check that pan,' she said, and went out to
the kitchen. Her mind was in too much of a tur-

moil to allow her to speak, or think rationally. She busied herself at the sink, finding pots that needed washing, a forgotten pan that should have had a good scrub, and giving it one. Anything to keep herself from having to think over what had just happened.

She heard him returning, and put the kettle on. Mrs. MacPhail drank pots and pots of tea every day, another would not come amiss now...

He was there, in the doorway, watching her. She turned sharply. 'Can I help you?' he asked.

'No. I'm just brewing more tea, then I'll be in. Go and talk to Mrs. MacPhail. She'll find you some more wool to wind if you ask her.' She felt as though she was babbling foolishly. She couldn't help herself. Something was happening that did not concern her, and she wanted to be sure that he understood. She added: 'I'll go back home and leave you here if you like. I have a lot of jobs to do.'

'Do you? Would you mind if I stayed?'

'I've just said so. There are some neighbours you can talk to as well. I'll tell them before I go if you want.'

'No, I'll manage that myself. When we've had the tea, I'll run you back home.'

'There's no need. I can walk.'

'Of course there's a need. It must be three miles. You can't walk with your foot. Here——' he came over to where she stood by the stove. 'I'll make the tea. Go and sit down.'

'Do you order everyone about like that?'

He grinned at her suddenly, surprisingly. 'Was I ordering you? *Please* go and sit down. Is that better?'

'You can't bully her, anyway,' Jan retorted. 'She had you winding wool before you'd got your breath. I'll bet that's a change for you.'

'Yes, it was.' He seemed almost amused.

Jan walked away from him, and went in to where the old lady waited, eyes alight with curiosity. She had good hearing. She must have heard their exchange. She motioned Jan over and took her hand. Whispering, she said: 'You don't get on?'

Jan looked down at her. What could she say? 'He's bossy,' she whispered back, uneasily aware that Mrs. MacPhail was too shrewd for comfort.

'Hmphm! I see. Well,' in a louder voice, 'sit you down, then. So you're away back to the house, are you? And how's your father?'

This was better. Jan sat down. 'He's fine—the same as ever, of course. He's doing something with a boat engine now—though we daren't ask what it is.'

The old lady snorted. 'He'll never change. Aye, well, as long as it keeps him happy. I've not seen him for a while. Give him my love, and tell him to come and visit me some time.'

'I will,' Jan promised. 'But you know him——'

'I do that. I'd visit you myself, but it's too far to walk at my age, with my leg.'

'Perhaps Breck would bring you up, while he's here——' and as she said it, he walked in, and, handing them their cups said:

'Of course. Any time. As long as you don't mind travelling in a Land-Rover?'

Mrs. MacPhail laughed. 'Ach, why not? You'll not go too fast, mind? I'm not as young as I was remember.'

'I'll drive so carefully you'd not even know you

were moving, I promise you that, Mrs. MacPhail.'

Jan drank her tea as quickly as she could. These two had established a kind of rapport in just an hour or so that disturbed her. 'Then I'll go now,' she said. 'You come up any time you like and have the day with us. Just as long as Breck tells me.' She looked at him. 'May we go now?'

He stood up. 'Yes. I'll be straight back, Mrs. MacPhail. I have a lot of questions to ask you—and get your wool ready. I'll do that too.' And he looked at Jan and smiled slightly.

As they neared Craigie House, he asked: 'Is there anything you need from the shop today?'

'No, thank you. Just leave me here.' She began to open her door, but it was jammed again, and he had to lean over and unfasten it.

'Can you manage?'

'Yes, thank you. What about lunch?'

'Oh, I can manage without. I'll be back later. Au revoir, Jan.' He gave her a mocking salute and began to reverse, to turn round and drive away again. She didn't answer, or look back. She walked slowly towards the front door, hearing the engine noise recede as he went away again, and then there was silence. She stood still before the entrance to her house, and looked about her. Utter silence, save for distant birds quarrelling in a tree. She had always been very content with her home and surroundings, but now there was a strange sad feeling filling her, as if of someone or something missing. She looked up at the gracious grey building smothered with ivy and wondered what it could be.

There was plenty to do, much to occupy her, and Jan busied herself that afternoon, but it was as though she were waiting for something. It was not until she heard the Land-Rover returning much later that she knew what it was.

Terry and Breck had a talk in the kitchen after dinner that night. Everything was cleared away, and Jan, her sisters, and their father were all in the sitting room, and both men had drifted off a short while before, excusing themselves by asking if it would be all right if they had a discussion about work—and could they make themselves coffee while they talked?

Mr. Sutherland, glasses perched on the end of his nose, was attempting *The Times* crossword. It was a lifetime ambition to complete it, and so far he had not succeeded. Judy and Helen were playing Scrabble, not without frequent cries of 'That's cheating!' and an occasional dive to the dictionary to confirm or deny the accusation.

Jan said brightly, and very casually: 'I'll make us all some coffee,' a remark which was completely ignored by the others. She went quietly out, along the corridor and opened the kitchen door. The air was blue with smoke, and two heads were bent over a large sheet of paper on the kitchen table.

Neither of the men looked up. 'No. There first—then along here.' Breck was tracing a path with his finger, and she saw that the paper was in fact a map of Dark Isle. She stood still for a moment by the door, and Terry's eyes met hers.

'Hello, Jan. Sorry, we were deep in shop talk. Are we in your way?'

'No. I've just come to make coffee. Don't disturb yourselves.'

Breck stubbed out a cigarette in the ashtray on the table. Two notebooks lay open, covered in writing. Then he looked up at Jan. 'Thanks for taking me to Mrs. MacPhail's,' he told her. 'She's been better than a dozen people to talk to.'

'I'm sure she has,' Jan answered. 'You were lucky she took to you. You'd have got nothing if she hadn't liked you.'

He grinned at Terry. 'I told you that, didn't I?' He stood up. 'Here, let me put the kettle on for you. Sit down—if you want to.' The last four words added in dry tones.

'I'll do it myself, thanks. I know how much water I need. Do you want coffee as well?'

'Please.' Breck began folding the map, putting it and the notebooks away. 'Will it be all right if our team arrives next Saturday? Then we can give them the day to settle in and look round. And start work in earnest the following Monday—a week to-day.'

'I suppose so.' Jan was busy with the kettle. 'And how long will you all be here after that?' she spoke very casually.

Terry answered, laughing. 'You should be shot of us all a couple of weeks later,' he said.

Three weeks. In three weeks they would all be gone; the camera crew, Terry, and Breck. Gone away back to London—and she wouldn't see him again. What a relief that would be! Jan smiled brightly and said: 'Want anything to eat, you two?'

'Not for me, thanks,' answered Breck. He was watching her, puzzled. 'What about you, Terry?'

'Nor me. Just coffee, thanks.

Breck looked at his watch. 'We'll come back in with you if we may. Time we showed our faces—and I did promise to help your father with any clues he was stuck on in the crossword.'

Jan laughed. 'I hope you're better than him,' she answered. 'He's never finished one yet.'

'We'll see. Jan, how's the bedding situation for weekend? I mean, will you be short? There'll be about four people coming, and we don't want——'

'We'll manage,' she answered. 'You've seen the size of the house. There are vast linen cupboards on one landing upstairs. The sheets and blankets might be rather old, but they're still good and warm.'

'Okay. We'll all get cracking whenever you say, and prepare the beds. Just let Terry and me know. We don't expect you and your sisters to do all the work.'

She felt herself go warm. Before she really thought about it, she answered:

'You're paying guests. We can't expect you to do everything for yourselves.' Breck looked at her, and she wished she could have bitten back the words, which had somehow come out more sharply than she intended. Terry murmured something which might have been: 'I'll just go and see——' and vanished.

They were alone now. Breck had a certain look on his face. Perhaps that was why Terry had gone. 'I *see*,' said Breck. 'Thanks for telling me.'

'I didn't mean——' she stopped. She wasn't sure now what she had meant.

'No,' he said, in a quite gentle tone. 'You're not always certain what you do mean, are you? Do you have to be so prickly when you're offered help?'

'I don't intend to start another argument with you,' she answered. 'Let me find some cups.' She walked past him, only she didn't get far, because he put his hand on her arm and stopped her.

'It's not me who starts them,' he pointed out. 'It's you. And you are the most exasperating female who——'

'Thanks,' she gritted. 'Will you let me go?'

'Not yet. I can't talk to you when you're darting about——'

'I can hardly dart about with a foot like mine,' she answered swiftly. 'Just take your hand *off my arm.*'

'Temper, temper!' Mocking, maddening, he spoke softly and quietly, and Jan put her fingers up to prise his hand away.

'Get *off* me,' she breathed. 'You bully!'

'Just listen for a minute. You never listen to anybody, you're so full of your own ideas, and what *you* want to say that no one gets a——'

She couldn't release his grip. Furiously she glared up at him. And he began to laugh. 'It's almost worth it,' he said, after a few moments, 'just to see you in a temper. You're quite something, you know—tell me, are you going to put on a performance like this for the cameras?'

'You won't get me near those!' she burst out. 'You must be joking!'

'Why not? You live here. We're featuring the house—and your father——'

'Not me, though. Just leave me out of it.'

'Mmm, I don't know,' he went on, almost as if she had not spoken. 'We could film you and one of your sisters playing tennis—just a casual, friendly game, like the one you and I had.'

Jan stopped trying to free herself. 'Well, I suppose you feel happier for getting *that* little dig off your chest,' she said. 'So now can I go?'

'In a moment. We will help you, you know. Just to prove we're not useless. You'll never get your ankle better if you don't rest it.'

'I will. I do rest it, as often as I can.'

'I hadn't noticed.'

'Your concern is touching,' she answered. 'You really should have been a doctor—you'd have done more good than what you're doing now.'

He lifted a cynical eyebrow. 'Lectures on my career now? What next, I wonder?'

She was silent. His nearness, despite everything, was very disturbing to her. Her heartbeats felt suffocatingly loud. She wanted to escape—and yet, in a strange way, she didn't. And she looked up and met his dark glance. His grey eyes were shadowed, mysterious, and she sensed the power within him, saw the hard lines of his expressive mouth soften momentarily as he murmured:

'What a girl!' His free hand reached out to touch her face, and she could scarcely breathe.

'Let me—go,' but the last word was lost as his lips came down on hers in a brief hard kiss that held no passion, only insult. Incensed, she tried to push him away and was imprisoned within the circle of his arms instantly. Helpless, overpowered, she jerked her head to escape further punishment and he took hold of her hair and held her completely helpless as he kissed her a second time. Harder still, ruthless—only this time something changed. Quite suddenly the kiss no longer hurt her. She found herself melting into a delirious response, found to her horror that she was enjoying it, discovered that the imprisoning arms that held her were not steel bands after all, but were warm and wonderful instead...

'So you see,' and his voice was husky, 'that's how I'll tame you, if I can't find any other way.' He was releasing her now, the kiss was over. It must have been her imagination that it had meant something to him as well, because his words were heavy with mockery as he turned away. She was free. Trembling, she found her voice.

'You are *hateful*,' she whispered.

'Am I? Good. I enjoy being hateful occasionally. Good for the manly image and all that.' But he wasn't really laughing, and the muscles tightened in his jaw as he moved from her. 'Hadn't you better make that coffee? The kettle's making a hell of a din.'

She hadn't even noticed. Jan made the coffee. How on earth, she wondered, as she set the cups out, and Breck stood at the window looking out into a starlit sky, how on earth could you find you were falling for a man you didn't even *like*? It should not have been possible, yet to her dismay she knew that that was precisely what was happening to her.

CHAPTER EIGHT

JAN lay awake for a long time that night. So many things were becoming clear to her now; her sudden feeling of loneliness that morning after Breck had left her; her sense of pain on hearing that in a few weeks he would have left Dark Isle for ever. Puzzling and disturbing at the time they happened, and now she knew why. Restlessly she turned and punched her pillow into shape. She couldn't even lie comfortably in bed, for her foot ached whichever way she put it, and she was far too warm.

Everybody else was asleep. The house was silent, bedroom doors shut. There was something else too; something she had put to the back of her mind because she had sensed at the time that it did not concern her. But now, in a way, it did; Breck's admission of who his grandparents had been.

The picture of old Mr. MacLeod came back clearly to her as she lay there looking at the ceiling. A tall grey-haired man with hawk nose and piercing dark eyes—Jan had always been slightly in awe of him as a child, until that day when she had fallen into the loch while her mother had been visiting Mrs. MacPhail. The old wooden jetty was out of bounds because it was rotten. Jan, with the curiosity of a child, had conveniently forgotten the ban and walked along it, the princess escaping from the pirates...

Terrified and crying, she had gone right down

when the wood gave way and felt the grey waters close over her head, forcing the breath from her body, seeing frightening green pictures as the greedy water sucked her down ... And then he had waded in and pulled her up, and out, and she had clung sobbing to him as he carried her into the house where her mother was busy talking. He had produced a hot spicy drink, herb-smelling and bitter, but she had drunk it, and the pain and fear had melted away for ever ... And that old man had been Breck's grandfather. Jan sighed. How strange life was! Like a pattern that could only be seen from far away...

It was no use. Sleep was as distant as ever. Further away, if that was possible, than when she had gone to bed. Flinging back the bedclothes, she pattered barefoot to the light and switched it on, and then lifted out the box with her writing in.

The words came easily, because the pent-up turbulence within her tumbled out on the paper to add richness to her efforts. She was not aware of this, only conscious that her pen was speeding over the exercise book, filling the blankness with words that gradually had the effect of making her feel tired. Soon the pen grew heavy, the lines blurred and danced and merged so that she had to blink. But there was a feeling of satisfaction at what she had done, and at last, when she knew her writing would be virtually unintelligible, Jan put down the book and pen, lay back, and with a little sigh fell asleep. With the light on.

Helen had been rather strange at breakfast. At first Jan put it down to her over-active imagination, but when at last they were alone in the kitchen doing the washing up, and Judy had set out on her bicycle to go to Mrs. MacPhail's, Jan knew that there was something amiss.

'Helen? Is anything the matter? Aren't you feeling well?'

Helen looked down at the plate she was drying and gave it a few unnecessary rubs. Her cheeks were faintly pink. 'Nothing's wrong,' she answered, but she wouldn't look up.

'But you hardly spoke at breakfast,' Jan said gently. 'And you didn't answer Breck or Terry when they said good morning—I'm sure Daddy noticed.'

'I saw him!' Helen burst out, and she looked up now, her eyes meeting Jan's at last. Eyes full of dismay.

'Saw who?'

Helen bit her lip. 'It's all right, it's none of my business, and I won't say anything, but oh, Jan, I thought you *hated* him!'

Jan clutched her forehead. 'One of us is going mad! I don't know what you're talking about. For heaven's sake tell me.'

Helen's face changed. 'You don't *know—honestly*?'

'Honestly. Cross my heart. Now, put that plate down before you rub the pattern off completely, sit down, and tell me.'

Helen did so. 'I was just going to the bathroom in the middle of the night,' she began, 'and I'd just opened my door when I heard a sound—a light going off—and then Breck walked out of your room, and closed the door very quietly after him.'

'But——' Jan gasped, 'I don't understand!' The horror in her eyes was only too real. She sat down beside Helen. 'I can't—are you sure you weren't mistaken?'

Helen shook her head. 'I saw him clearly. He didn't see me. He went to his room and closed the door, so I waited a few minutes, then went to the bathroom. I felt *sick*. Oh, Jan, I'm sorry—I thought——'

'Yes, well, never mind that.' Jan stood up. 'What was he doing in my room? Let me think for a moment.' She remembered writing, putting the exercise book on her table when she was too tired to do any more. And the next thing that had happened was that she had woken up. She looked down at Helen. 'Where is he?' she said.

'Upstairs as far as I know. Terry's gone in the Land-Rover to the shop. I gave him that list you made out——'

'Good. Stay here and finish the dishes. I'm going to see Breck Fallon.' Her mouth was set in a determined line, and Helen watched her go, then picked up a cup from the draining board.

'I'd like a word with you,' Jan said. 'In private.'

'Then you'd better come in, hadn't you?' Breck's tone was mild. He looked up from his open case, then at the sight of Jan's face, closed the lid slowly and straightened up from his crouching position.

'What were you doing in my room in the middle of the night?'

For a moment he looked blank, and then a broad grin spread across his face. 'Oh,' he said. 'So that's it! How did you know?'

'Never mind how I knew.' He hadn't tried to deny it. Jan fought for control from the confused sensation that filled her. 'What were you——?'

'All right, don't ask again, I heard you perfectly

well the first time.' He crossed the room to where she stood and pushed the door shut behind her. 'Right, *Miss* Jan—you can wipe that furious look from your face for a start. Because what I was doing in *your* room wasn't what you so clearly think.'

'You don't know what I was thinking!' she retorted.

'Oh, don't I? Considering that outraged virtue is written all over you I've got a damn good idea! Believe me, if I'd gone in with the intention of seducing you, you wouldn't be wondering, you'd *know*.'

'You have no right——' she began, warmth creeping up from her neck and into her cheeks.

'Oh yes, I have! Shut up and listen. I saw your light on when I went to the bathroom about four a.m. It was still on when I came out, so I went over to your door and called your name quietly. I thought you might be ill. There was no answer, and the door was ajar, so I pushed it open and looked in. You were fast asleep with the light on, your exercise book at your bedside, and half your bedclothes over the floor.'

He stopped and looked at her. 'What? No interruptions? So I picked up the sheets and covered you up, switched off the lights and came out.' Jan closed her eyes. She remembered putting the book down, lying back, and the light had been on. It had not been on when she woke up.

'Helen saw you,' she said dully. 'She thought——'

'Mmm, I'm sure she did. I'll go and explain.' He moved to the door.

'No, I'll do it.' It seemed that an apology might be in order. 'I'm sorry I——' she began, but wasn't allowed to finish.

'Don't apologise. I wouldn't expect that from you!' His eyes gleamed. 'I'm only sorry I disappointed you—after all, you like to think the worst of me at all times——'

'With some justification!' she retorted, all thoughts of admitting her mistake vanishing at his tone, 'after your brutal attack yesterday——' it was easier to sound full of righteous indignation when she had firmly quashed all those guilty memories of the sheer enjoyment...

'Brutal attack! What on *earth* are you talking about?'

He couldn't have forgotten, could he? Jan, wide-eyed with astonishment, could hardly speak. 'You—you——' she began. 'When you *kissed* me.'

'Oh, that!' He looked down at her, then began to laugh softly. 'No wonder you write stories, with that vivid imagination! Still, I bet you'll use it in your book. *I'd* forgotten. You really mustn't take everything so seriously——'

Humiliation filled her. He hadn't remembered. 'Seriously? You must be joking!' she managed, with an effort. It was very important that he never guessed the bitter truth. She struggled to find words. 'You're not in London now, you conceited *beast*. I dare say you can go round kissing who you want and no one even *notices*, but we're not like that here, thank you. Men here have respect for women. They don't treat them like you do. The sooner you go away, the better it will be for all of us.' The reckless words poured out willy-nilly in a tumbling confusion, and why he should find it so amusing she had no idea, but she hated him for it. Her breast heaved, eyes sparked fire at him, and

she stood there tall and slender, completely unaware that her angry mood only served to increase
her beauty. But then she saw something in his eyes
—a sudden response, although she didn't recognize
it—and it frightened her so that she turned quickly
away. She had said too much.

'Don't go,' he said. 'I'm enjoying this tirade.
Your choice of words is fascinating——' and he
caught her arm.

'Oh no, you don't! Not again!' She lashed out
wildly. 'You're not touching me again.' Her flying
hand caught his arm and he moved slightly sideways, grinning broadly.

'Wow! What a temper! I shouldn't think any
man here could get near you, never mind trying to
kiss you. You certainly scare me.' But he didn't
look frightened—only as if he was taking a delight
in taunting her. Jan felt like throwing something
at him. She stood there, loathing him, wondering
why she had ever imagined she could be feeling a
treacherous warmth towards him. He was hateful!
And because there seemed no way that she could
ever get the better of him, and because his mockery
touched her on the raw, she said: 'I'm sorry you
ever met Diane—do you hear me? I wish you
hadn't! You wouldn't have come here then, up-
setting everything——' And she suddenly knew
something else, in a blinding moment of awareness.
'It was only because your grandparents lived here
too—*that* was the real reason. I saw your face in
Mrs. MacPhail's when you looked at the photograph. You didn't like them, did you?' She saw his
face change, and darken, saw his eyes become
darker too, and knew she had gone too far. But she
couldn't stop now. Some force made her go, reck-

lessly, frighteningly, as she burst out: 'Well, *I* liked them! I don't care about you—your grandfather was a good man, respected by everyone here——'

His voice cut in deep and angry, stopping her words. 'You know *nothing*,' he grated. 'Nothing. So be quiet about things that don't concern you——'

'I won't be quiet! Everything here concerns me——' she gasped as he took hold of her upper arms and gripped her tightly. 'Ow! Let me go!'

'Then shut up. I'm not discussing it with you.' And he stood there looking down at her, holding her with such power that she was afraid of him, and his grey eyes were nearly black with hidden anger. Her own temper melted rapidly. Gone the desire to wipe the mockery from his eyes—she wanted now only to get away from him, but she couldn't. He was too strong.

'Take your hands off me,' she whispered. There was pain in his eyes too, mixed up with the anger, a combination she didn't understand—only that her words had triggered it off. 'I hate you!'

He took his hands away from her arms. Jan stumbled back and put her hand to her mouth to stifle a sob of fear and pain. He didn't move. He seemed hardly aware of her presence. She turned and walked out of the room.

Work was the only antidote to the anguish that filled her. Breck had turned into a virtual stranger, coldly polite when it was inevitable that they had to speak. For the rest of the day she avoided him as much as possible, and it was not difficult for he and Terry went out in the Land-Rover soon afterwards, taking Judy with them, after asking her if she would show them certain parts of the island. The change in Judy was unbelievable. She had brushed her dark hair until it shone, and wore a clean pair of jeans and tee shirt, and her mouth was a delicate pink with what looked suspiciously like lipstick.

Helen and Jan were cleaning in the living room when they went. Helen stood by the window as Jan busily polished the vast sideboard beside it. 'It's Terry,' she announced. 'That's what's done it. She looks at him all soppy! Honestly, I never thought it possible.'

Jan didn't answer. She was rubbing very hard on the polished surface, making it shine. 'And what's up with Breck?' Helen added thoughtfully. 'He barely spoke to me when I asked him how long they'd be. I only wanted to know because of lunch,' she said, 'but he practically *glared* at me. Aren't men strange? Is he annoyed because I saw him leaving your room?'

Jan sighed. 'I don't think it's that,' she answered. 'If it's any consolation, he's not speaking to me either. I'm glad,' she added. 'He's absolutely *awful*,' and she bent with renewed vigour to her task, and missed the look that Helen gave her.

She had an idea later that evening, and went out into the kitchen to tell the two men, who were once more talking out there. She stood at the door for a moment, and saw Breck's profile before he turned round to her.

Strength and hardness was there—and something else she didn't understand, and she wished that she had not said the words she had—but it was too late.

'I'm sorry,' he said, icy cool. 'Are we in the way here?'

'No, but it's why I've come. It's not practical you using this kitchen when the others arrive. You need a proper room to work and talk in. There's another sitting room you haven't seen. If you'd like to come and take a look now, we can get it prepared for the weekend.'

He stood up, followed by Terry. It was obvious that Terry knew something was very must amiss, but he was his smiling self, and he grinned warmly at Jan. 'Good idea,' he said. 'Though I'm getting quite fond of my kitchen. You'll still let me cook, won't you?'

Jan smiled. 'Of course. This way.' She could walk quite easily now, and each day her foot grew stronger. She opened the door into the room at the other side of the front of the house, and a wave of cold air met them. 'You see,' she said as they went in. 'It will need airing and cleaning, but there's lots of space—and a good sized table. You could keep the cameras and things'—she waved vaguely round her—'in here too.'

'It seems ideal,' Breck said. 'What say you, Terry?'

'Fine.' He walked to the empty fireplace. 'What an enormous room. You don't use it at all?'

'Not now,' Jan answered. 'So you can have it all the time, while you're here.' She looked round. 'I'll do it in the morning and light the fire, then you can both bring your stuff in. I'll tell my sisters not to come in at all.'

Breck stuck his hands in the pockets of his jacket. 'Thanks. There's just one thing. I've got a portable television in my room. Have I your permission to plug that in here, and have it on?'

Jan felt herself go cold. The dry irony in his tone

spoke volumes. Yet there was nothing she could do about it. She just wondered vaguely why Helen had never mentioned seeing *that* when she had gone to dust his room.

'Of course.' She had vowed that there would never be one of those things in the house, but to refuse would have made her seem incredibly childish.

She turned away. 'Well, that's fixed, then. I just thought I'd show you now.' But she wondered, when she went back to join her father and sisters, if he had ever had it switched on in his room.

She should have known what would happen. The three girls had begun cleaning the room after breakfast the following morning, and Terry had insisted on coming in to move any heavy furniture around, and had ended up making paper firelighters with Judy while Jan and Helen dusted and wiped round the paintwork. And Breck walked in while they were thus engrossed, bearing books and folders full of papers.

'All right to leave these on the table?' he asked Jan, his tone still cool and formal.

'Yes, it's been cleaned.'

He went out again. A few minutes later he came back carrying a portable television. Judy and Helen looked at each other, then at Jan.

He seemed unaware of any atmosphere, merely said: 'That small table by the window—may I put it on that? It won't scratch it.'

'Yes.' Her voice felt stiff.

'Thanks.' Helen had quite frankly stopped her polishing in mid-sweep and was watching in fascination, while Judy picked up another sheet of newspaper and said to Terry:

'I'll go and get the coal in a minute.'

'No, let me. If you'll show me where it is, I'll bring it in.'

'Oh well, it's in the cellar,' she replied, and unblushingly added: 'It is a bit heavy.'

Jan heard Helen's faint snort, but ignored it. They're all going mad, she thought. But there was worse to come, later.

Breck spent the next few minutes plugging in, adjusting the aerial and twiddling with switches, and suddenly there was background music, and voices, and a blurred picture appeared on the screen.

'Terry, come and hold this, will you?' Breck frowning, knelt and began to turn the knobs, and handed Terry the aerial. 'Back a bit—no, higher. That's it. Hold it!'

The picture sharpened instantly, the aerial was put carefully on to the end of the mantelpiece, and they all stood watching—even Jan. She had only ever seen one television set on at her aunt Ina's, and that reluctantly. But this was in brilliant colour, clearly a schools programme, for a woman was cutting bright pieces of paper into animal shapes, watched by a group of youngsters. Breck left it on and walked away from it. He was well aware of the reaction, Jan knew. The room was nearly ready.

'Right, Judy,' she said briskly. 'Why don't you go and get that coal now with Terry? Then the fire can be lit. Helen, go in the kitchen, I'll be with you in a minute, and we'll get lunch ready.'

'But I've not——' Helen began.

'Yes, you have.'

Then there were just the two of them in the

room, Jan and Breck. She turned to him. 'I hope you're pleased with yourself,' she said softly.

He looked up from the table, where he was bending over open books. 'I beg your pardon?' he answered.

She pointed to the set. 'You know what I mean,' she retorted. 'You did it deliberately.'

'I asked your permission—remember? And you gave it.'

'There was no need to switch it on now.' She rubbed a chair vigorously.

'You're letting your prejudices show,' he answered, smoothly, swiftly. 'Or are you afraid your sisters might actually enjoy it?' When she didn't answer, he went on: 'Perhaps they're not allowed to have opinions of their own, is that it?'

'Not at all,' she said crisply. 'They feel as I do about television.'

'You wouldn't put it to the test, though, would you?' he asked, and then Jan realized the trap. She looked at him, unable to speak, turned and walked out and closed the door behind her. But not quickly enough to miss the mocking laugh.

Breck came out into the kitchen after dinner that evening. A pile of washing up was stacked on the working top next to the sink, and she was filling the bowl with water.

'I'll help you,' he said.

'I don't need anything from you,' she answered. 'Especially not your help. You've done enough today.' Eyes dark with suppressed anger, she looked at him.

'It's hardly my fault if your father found there was a programme on about astronomy,' he pointed out. 'Nor that your sisters decided to watch it with him. What would you have me do? Scream and shout like you would, and tell them they couldn't watch my television?'

'You made sure he found out about it.' She was fighting to speak calmly, but with difficulty. 'You planned it all very carefully.'

'You gave us the room. It wasn't my idea.' He was standing quite near her, very tall and over-powering and invulnerable. That was what disturbed her so much, his utter *strength*. Jan hadn't known many men. Her father was always so gentle and kind, the islanders she met in her day-to-day life courteous and thoughtful—and now this man had entered her life and turned it upside down. Because he was hard and ruthless and quite intent on getting his own way. And even as she thought this, he picked up a tea towel and said: 'Right, off we go, then.'

'I said I didn't need your help,' she said, very clearly and slowly, and put a pile of dirty dinner plates in the soapy water and began to rub them with the dishcloth.

'But I don't take no for an answer—or hadn't you noticed?' he said. 'So apart from chucking me bodily out of the kitchen—a feat of which you are not capable—there's very little you can do about it. And why don't you stop being so childish?'

'It is not childish to want to be alone occasionally,' she answered. 'Nor to prefer to do tasks without your assistance. You go out of your way to be rude. Are you like this with everyone you work with? I'll bet they were glad to get rid of you in London.' And she stacked the plates neatly on the draining board. He picked two of them up, and began to dry them.

'No, I'm not. It's only you who brings out the worst in me,' he answered. 'I wonder why?'

'I don't care. Just stay out of my way and leave me alone.' She flashed an angry glance at him and he put the plates down and lifted his hand to her face. For a dreadful moment she thought he was going to strike her, and she flinched instinctively and he laughed.

'I was just going to see if your cheeks were as hot as they look,' he said. 'You have two angry spots burning away. Did you think I was going to kiss you or something?'

She moved his hand away. 'No,' she said shortly. 'I thought you were going to hit me.'

'Now why would I want to do that?' he seemed almost amused. But it was there all right—the tension, building up between them as it always did when they were alone. Crackling electric antagonism, filling the room, making her breathless and unsure of herself.

She shook her head, incapable of speech. There was a certain release in rubbing the cups and plates in the hot soapy water. Breck picked up another dish and looked at it. 'Hmm, lost for words again. That's getting very worrying—not like you at all.'

Oh, I hate you, how I hate you, she thought. You are cruel and full of mockery, and why does it hurt so? Silence was her only refuge. Whatever she said, he had an answer. Whatever she did, he was one move ahead, waiting, teasing, like a cat tormenting its victim. She took a deep breath, and it came out like a sigh, and he said: 'Why don't you admit when you're beaten?'

Jan turned her head and looked at him. Her

dark eyes were bright, too bright, because they glistened with unshed tears. She heard his sharp in-drawn breath, saw his own eyes darken as he looked back at her, and at that same moment a vivid flash of lightning filled the room with blue-white elec-tric brilliance—followed only seconds later by the most deafening roar and crack of thunder. She dropped the plate she was holding on to the floor, and her head jerked back in fear. And he put his arms round her instinctively—and Jan found the strength to push back at him. The explosive crackle had broken the tension.

'Leave me,' she cried. 'Leave me *alone*!' Jerking herself free, she ran from him, fleeing from the kitchen as if pursued, running up the stairs to her room, foot aching, but not stopping for anything. She was sobbing now, not because of the storm, be-cause they didn't bother her, but because of what she had seen in his eyes, the moment before that blinding flash of light. No man had ever looked at her like that before. She was disturbed—and fright-ened. And she knew that she must not be alone with Breck Fallon again.

CHAPTER NINE

JAN kept herself very busy the next couple of days —and avoided Breck as much as possible. He was busy anyway, in the room she had given to him and Terry to work in, and there was much washing and ironing to be done in preparation for the camera team's arrival on Friday. Jan's nerves were ragged. She felt irritable and restless, and even Terry's ever cheerful banter failed to restore her good spirits.

Breck too seemed silent and introspective, and once, as she passed their room, she heard him and Terry in what sounded like an argument. She hurried past unwilling to listen, telling herself she didn't care anyway.

Later that day, Friday, Terry said to her in the kitchen: 'I don't know what's the matter with Breck, he snapped my head off today. I'll be glad when the others arrive.' She looked at him, and he grinned. 'Sorry, don't take any notice of me, Jan.'

'Oh, but I do. You're always so happy, Terry. Don't let him get you down.'

He laughed. 'Oh, I won't. He'll be different tomorrow, you see. We just have a lot on at the moment, that's all.'

But he was wrong there. On Saturday morning Breck left the house mid-morning and Terry came out into the kitchen where Jan was busily preparing lunch and said: 'Let me help. I need a break.'

'Have a coffee first,' she suggested. 'What's the matter?'

He went to fill the kettle. 'He's just slammed out to go and see Mrs. MacPhail——' at Jan's look of alarm, he said quickly: 'No, don't worry, he'll be all right with *her*, honestly—but he's going round like a bear with a sore head. I can do nothing right at the moment. God, we've never known him so grouchy.' He looked at her shrewdly. 'Have you any idea why?'

She turned from rolling out pastry. 'Me? What do you mean, Terry?' but her heart beat faster at his expression.

He shrugged. 'Nothing, only——' and he paused, and looked worriedly at the cooker. 'Nothing—forget I spoke.'

'I can't,' she said gently. 'Tell me what you meant—please.'

'Well, have you had a row or anything?'

Jan stopped her pastry rolling completely. 'We have nothing else,' she answered simply. 'Or hadn't you noticed?'

'Yes, I had.' He looked extremely uncomfortable. 'Oh, heck, I'm sorry—it's nothing to do with me, but——'

'But?'

'Well, I've never seen him behave like this with any woman before. I don't know why, I'm sure.'

Jan let out her breath sharply. 'We detest one another, it's as plain as that.'

He grimaced. 'And it's absolutely nothing to do with me—so why don't you tell me to mind my own business?'

She smiled at him. 'I couldn't do that. You're too nice, Terry.'

He bowed. 'Thank you for those kind words. Now I feel better.' He laughed, his normal high spirits restored. 'Oh, I like you, Jan. What say we do something really superb for a sweet today?'

She changed her mood to match his. 'Right. We'll have a look what we've got, shall we? And not think about anything except food!' And she tried hard, she really did, but it was very difficult to put the man called Breck Fallon from her mind—impossible, in fact. He was always there. Always.

It would be better, she knew, when the others came.

They arrived late on Saturday afternoon in pouring rain. Three men and a girl, and they came in a van loaded with equipment that was all carefully unloaded and taken into their room; cameras, and microphones and recording machine and their own luggage, together with rolls of film and cardboard boxes...

Breck had gone with Terry in the Land-Rover to meet them from the ferry, and he went to the kitchen after the offloading was finished, and said to Jan:

'Can I get them all a cup of tea?'

They hadn't spoken all day, not one word. 'I've put the kettle on,' she answered. 'I'll bring it in to you in a few minutes, when it's made,' and she turned her back to him, and went on with what she was doing. There was a moment's silence, then she heard him walk out.

She brewed the tea, set out six beakers, sugar and milk on a try, and carried it all in.

The room was transformed. No longer a rather dull sitting room, it resembled a hive of industry as six people, one of them female, bent over a map of Dark Isle on the table, and six voices all tried to speak at once. Jan's heart thudded. They all looked so casual—and somehow hard. She was glad that Terry was there, that it was he who saw her first, and came over to take the tray from her and say in a raised voice:

'Come and meet the crew, Jan.' The voices died away. Four heads swivelled round, four pairs of eyes looked at her. Breck was too engrossed in the chart to look up. Jan smiled, trying to hide her nervousness.

'Hello, Jan,' the girl said, and grinned. Tall and thin, she had discarded a grey mackintosh to reveal a jazzy shirt and blue jeans.

'Hello,' Jan answered.

'Deirdre—commonly known as Dee, because for some reason she doesn't like her name,' Terry said, as the two girls shook hands.

Dee pulled a face. 'Would *you* like it?' she asked. 'No, don't answer.' She had an engaging grin, short fair hair, and bright blue very round glasses perched on the end of her nose. Jan liked her instantly.

'And Bill—you have to watch him—Jack—Tom,' Terry went on, and Jan had a blurred impression of the three men who were here to stay for another couple of weeks. The first opinion—of their hardness—melted away instantly in the casual warmth of their greetings, and as they helped themselves to the tea, murmuring thanks, she was able to take them in as individuals. Bill was lean and lanky, in his thirties, Jack younger, smoking a pipe, with a shock of red hair, Tom in his mid-twenties with a studious look which was helped by the black horn-rimmed glasses he wore.

'I'll come out and help you get dinner ready,' Terry said, with a brief look at Breck.

'Let me,' Dee offered, and Jan was startled by a chorus of groans from the others.

'Please—no!' begged Jack, and Bill added:

'You're far too valuable here, Dee,' to which Dee retorted, her eyes sparkling:

'What you mean is, you don't think I can cook. Why don't you say it?'

'We don't think you can cook,' rose instantly from three male throats, followed by a roar of laughter.

Dee looked at Jan. 'Honestly,' she said. 'I could hit them sometimes! They'll never let me forget a certain incident—can I come and see your kitchen and tell you about it? I'd rather drink my tea out there—I don't think I like the company here very much.'

'Of course. Come on,' Jan led the way out, and into the kitchen. Dee put her beaker on the table.

'Gosh, that's better. I'm going to like it here. Can I see where I'm sleeping after?'

'Yes. I've given you the room next to mine. My two younger sisters have moved in together, and you've got Helen's room.'

'I hope I'm not putting you out,' Dee said anxiously.

'No,' Jan shook her head. 'When Terry told me a girl was coming too, I rearranged things a little. Why don't they want you to cook?'

Dee laughed. 'It's more a joke than anything. I must confess I'm not the world's best—but just because we were once stuck in a remote village and I did them sausage and chips, and they got rather burnt'—she frowned—'well, they were pretty awful, I must admit—they won't let me near a cooker now.' She sighed. 'I don't really care. I'm not the domesticated type anyhow. Though I should be, as I'm a country girl at heart. I was brought up on a farm in the Lake District. This is like home from home to me.' She stretched luxuriously, like a supple cat. 'I shall enjoy this assignment. How do you get on with Breck and Terry?'

The question caught Jan off balance. She nearly spilt the tea she was pouring out for herself. 'Oh, Terry's fine.' And she stopped.

'Ah!' A slow grin spread across Dee's face. 'Did I make a boob? Sorry, love. You'll get used to me, sooner or later. I'm always opening my mouth and wishing I hadn't a minute after.' She seemed anxious to reassure Jan. 'If it's any consolation, I couldn't *stand* Breck the first time I worked with him. I thought he was the bossiest, most arrogant man I'd ever met——'

'But I didn't mean——' Jan began, then tailed away as she realized that Dee had discovered in just a few seconds exactly what she *did* mean.

'Look, we'll drop the subject if you prefer. Honest. Is there a drop more tea, please, Jan?'

'Yes, of course.' Jan smiled at Dee. 'What exactly do you do? Are you one of the camera team?'

Dee laughed. 'More a general dogsbody. I follow them around—and generally see that the people we're interviewing are sitting in the right place, and check things are going smoothly. Officially I'm a continuity girl, but between you and me I work far harder than those men,' here she winked slowly. 'Not that they'd accept that for a moment. But it's the truth.'

'I'm sure it is.' Jan's spirits lightened. When

Terry had said that one of the crew would be a girl, she had been worried. But she hadn't known why, except that perhaps it was because she feared a supercilious, sophisticated Londoner. And something else too, that she would hardly admit to herself—the faint, disturbing fear that she would be someone with whom Breck was in love...

Absurd, of course, because it didn't matter, not one jot—but the sensation of relief was quite overwhelming, and Jan smiled warmly at Dee as she poured her some more tea. 'It's always the way, isn't it?' she said. 'Men think they're so clever at everything, and they're not really.'

'I think we're going to get along just fine,' Dee confided. 'I can come and pour out all my troubles to you. It's fun being the only girl on an assignment usually, but oh, it's nice to have another girl to talk to.' And she raised her beaker. 'Cheers!' she said.

The house was strangely empty on Monday when they had all gone. They had taken sandwiches, and would be out all day, Terry told Jan before they went. But they would be back for dinner at about seven, if that was all right with her? Jan had assured him that it would be, and they had left.

There was plenty to do. Both Judy and Helen had been completely won over, and nothing was too much trouble for them, and the house was tidy in record time every day since the arrival of the crew. Things, Jan reasoned to herself, would never be the same again when they had finally departed. For more reasons than one...

After their own quick lunch, both Judy and Helen had departed on their bicycles to see the team in action. Jan, who secretly longed to go, had resisted the temptation and stayed behind at home with the excuse that her foot was not yet strong enough for cycling. Her father had gone out to the loch, taking with him the weird-looking contraption that was possibly going to revolutionize motorboat engines. The house was completely and utterly silent. Jan thought about writing, but the idea did not appeal. She was too restless in her mind to concentrate on putting words down on paper.

She had seen something in the morning paper that she had instantly dismissed as impossible, but now, as she stood in the guests' sitting room, checking that it was tidy, and looked across at the television in the corner, the memory of what she had read came back to her. There was a James Bond film on, and Jan had once read several of the books, and wondered how they could possibly translate his incredible adventures to the screen...

It would only be for a few minutes that she would look. Just to *see* ... That was *all*. She switched on, repressing a guilty twinge as she did so, and sat down on a stool to watch.

She had forgotten that it would be in colour, she had never heard the catchy theme music that now assailed her ears—and she had never even heard of Sean Connery who was playing James Bond. It was a fascinating world into which she was transported instantly, and somehow the five minutes had passed, then fifteen, only now Jan had forgotten to look at her watch as she gazed enraptured at the small screen, and heard an oddly familiar voice say:

'So this is what you do when everyone's out.' She

whirled round and nearly fell off the stool. Breck was standing just inside the doorway. Her face flamed, and he walked in. He wasn't laughing. He didn't seem remotely amused as he looked down at her.

'Aren't you the little hypocrite?' he remarked. 'You really take the biscuit.'

Jan stood up. 'I was curious,' she said.

'So you got rid of your sisters and settled down to enjoy a good film in peace and quiet. Yes, I see.'

'I didn't get rid of them!' she flared indignantly. 'They wanted to go and see you at work, and I came in to see that everything was tidy—and——' her voice trailed away. Why make excuses? The expression on his face was one she didn't like at all.

'Then don't let me disturb you,' he answered. 'I only came back for a spare recording machine. I'll go in a minute and you can watch undisturbed.'

'I don't want to, now,' she replied. 'Thank you,' and she made as if to walk past him, but he caught hold of her arm.

'Ah—ah! Temper! Just because you've been caught red-handed, there's no need to get all indignant with *me*—it won't wash. I shan't tell anyone, don't worry. It will be our little secret,' and he smiled—slowly. She didn't like the smile on him, or his television for that matter. Nor did she like him holding her. And it all flared up in one glorious moment of white-hot temper as she violently swung her arm round and struck him hard on the side of his face.

There was an electrifying moment of silence in which the slap seemed to echo and re-echo in the tension-filled room. He let out his breath, and said: 'And I told you what I would do if you *ever* hit me again.' She had never heard any voice so angry in her life. Fear lent her strength. She wrenched herself free and, gasping with shock, ran out of the room. Up the stairs, along the corridor—could she reach her room and lock the door before he caught up with her?

She heard his steps pounding up after her and desperately launched herself at her door, swung it open, her breath ragged now, sheer terror filling her.

And he was there, behind her even as she tried to push the door to, slamming it wide open, a furiously angry man who was going to—'No!' she cried. 'No, don't—ah, please—I'm sorry——'

'Too late.' The whiplash of his words filled the room. It was as if he too was on the point of explosion. All the pent-up silence of the previous few days, the friction, caused merely by their presence with each other, the atmosphere building to its slow smouldering climax—all these things were there in his eyes as he stood before her. This was no longer just the clash of personalities—this went far deeper than mere dislike.

He was a man at the end of his tether—and she knew that it was because of her, knew it as surely as she now knew that life, when this hateful, disturbing, vibrant man had gone, would be unbearable. His face was drawn, as if he had not slept. A change had come over him in the past few days and the others all knew it too, but they didn't know why.

Jan did, and now the moment of truth had arrived, and with the realization, a kind of fatalistic calm came over her. He reached out to grasp her arm, cruelly, bitingly, and she shuddered, and in a voice that didn't sound like her own, said:

'Get it over quickly.' Her whole body trembled, but she stood tall and straight, and she would not cry out, she would not. And she waited, and his hand burned like fire on her arm—and then she was pulled towards him, and his hard mouth came down on hers in one violent kiss of deep shattering passion...

The room whirled round in an explosion of stars. There was no strength in her at all, her body melted into quivering acquiescence at the force within him, communicating itself to her, filling her with tumultuous multi-coloured sensations, whirling round and round in a dizzying spiral—and then he released her, pushing her away from him, and she staggered back helplessly, seeing his eyes as she had never seen them before, black, unfathomable, tortured...

He turned away from her and went to the door. There were no words to be said. She knew that he could not speak, nor would he if he could, for some things are beyond words.

He went out. Jan sat on the bed, for her legs would not support her, and put her head in her hands. She heard Breck go downstairs, heard, after a minute, the front door close, and then the sound of the Land-Rover dying away.

After a few minutes she went to the bathroom and poured a long glass of cold water and drank it thirstily. Then, walking slowly, she went downstairs again.

And then, after a few days, it was the turn of Craigie House, and instead of going out every morning, Breck would be there all the time. Dee came out into the kitchen on Saturday and sat down, long legs crossed, glasses perched on the end of her nose, and she sighed. 'This will be a good room to film,' she said, looking round with an appraising eye. 'Bags of character, that lovely high window.' She put her hands up, making them in the rough shape of a television screen, and moved her head slowly round as if using a camera, a thoughtful frown on her forehead. 'Hmm, yes. We'll have you working at the table——'

Jan had hardly smiled for days, but she managed one now. 'Not me,' she said. 'I'm not going on. And since when have you been in charge?'

'A girl can dream, can't she?' was the indignant answer. 'And why won't you be filmed?' Dee sat up straight. 'You'll be very telegenic.'

'What does that mean? It sounds like some awful disease.'

'Same as photogenic, silly. Or translated, you should look super on the screen.'

Jan looked at her in dismay, expecting to see a teasing look on the other girl's face, but she wore a serious expression as she went on: 'Why won't you?'

'Didn't they tell you?' Jan tried to speak casually.

'Hmm—well, Terry did say something about you not liking telly, but I thought he was making it up. You don't, do you? Hate it, I mean? You don't hate us?'

'No,' Jan shook her head, smiling slowly. 'Of course not. I like you all. Well——' she hesitated, then, hurriedly: 'But I always said I'd never have a television here, it's too involved to go into now, Dee, but that's just the way I feel.'

Dee shrugged. 'It's a free world, I always say.

Hey, can I ask you something personal?' And without waiting for Jan's answer, she went on: 'Have you and Breck had a big row?'

Jan looked at her. She ached to tell someone, if only to assuage the pain. But what a strange question. Was it so obvious to everyone? She felt herself go warm. She sat down slowly opposite Dee. She sensed that she could trust the girl. Something must have showed in her eyes, some of the anguish, and Dee leaned forward, and said softly: 'I'm sorry, Jan, I shouldn't have asked. But he's acting so strange, and I thought——' she bit her lip.

'What did you think?'

'When I first came, I saw him looking at you once, when you were talking. No one else noticed, but I did—and there was something in his eyes that made me think——' she hesitated, then shook her head. 'I can't explain it exactly, that look. It was like—like——' she took a long breath. 'A depth I hadn't seen before to him. Just for a few moments it lasted, but it was enough—it was as though it lasted for ever. It's never happened again, but I couldn't forget it if I tried.'

'No. It's all right, Dee, I know what you mean. He hates me—he frightens me——'

'No—it wasn't like——'

'Yes, it was. I know. Believe me.' And quickly, jerkily, she began to tell the other girl exactly what had happened on their first meeting in the pouring rain, and the tennis—and other things. But not everything. There were some things she could not talk about to anyone in the world. But she told enough, and when she was finished, Dee let out her breath in a long sigh.

'You mustn't tell anyone, Dee. Promise me. I

know I can trust you.'

'Yes, you can. No wonder—oh, it explains a lot. What an absolute swine he is!'

'That's one way of describing him, I suppose. But, Dee, you mustn't let it affect your working relationship with him. I'd hate that. I only told you because I had to tell someone or burst.'

'I know, love, and don't worry—it won't. When we're working, personal feelings don't enter into it. We've all got a job to do, and we do it.' Dee shook her head. 'It's incredible, though. He's the last one I would have thought——' she checked herself abruptly as the door opened, and Helen came in.

'Breck's asking for you, Dee,' she told her.

Dee stood up, and winked at Jan. 'Then I must go. See you later, Jan.'

'Yes. Later.' Jan watched her go with mixed feelings. She wondered if she had done the wrong thing in confiding in another. She had always been able to work out her problems by herself in the past. But this was different. Because nothing like Breck Fallon had ever happened to her before.

Jan's father had the ability to surprise everyone. She and her sisters had been sure that when it actually came to it, he would be too shy to want to appear in front of television cameras, and would make excuses and generally procrastinate to such an extent that they would give up any ideas of filming him at work.

He revelled in the whole situation. It was almost, Jan thought, like seeing another man, instead of the vague, gentle scholarly father they had known all their lives. His walk became brisker, his voice more authoritative—in short, he was enjoying himself immensely, and it showed.

On Saturday afternoon it was decided to film him at the loch, working on the motor-boat engine he was perfecting, and they all set out mid-afternoon to do so. The light was good; Dee assured Jan that it was ideal for outdoor shooting, and that with any luck they would 'have it in the can' within a few hours. Jan was gradually getting used to the expressions used by the camera team, and to understand them. She watched them go, and the temptation was too great. The loch was only a short walk away, all the daily tasks were done, and the house seemed to echo with its emptiness.

Slipping on a dark blue jacket over her sweater and jeans, Jan set off to watch them all at work. Gulls wheeled overhead as she neared the water. Disturbed by the unusual amount of activity at their normally quiet spot, they were showing their objection in the only possible way, with harsh sad cries.

The van was parked on level ground before the downward slope to the shingly beach. Jan stood by it for a moment watching the activity below, and the scene was sharply etched in her brain because it was like nothing she had ever seen.

Her father was standing by their boat, the strange-looking contraption that was his new motor beside it. Dee was moving towards him bearing a large important-looking board with papers clipped on it, and Bill, Jack, Tom, and Terry were talking in a huddle with Breck. The hand cameras that they were using were laid on a trestle table which was also full of rolls of film, papers, and boxes. A large gull stood by it watching the scene with beady alert eyes. And Judy and Helen sat on a grassy bank and whispered together.

And at the precise moment that Jan decided to walk over to them, Breck looked up from the small group of men. His eyes met Jan's and held them in a long stare. It was, for a few seconds in time, as if there were no one else there. Everything faded into insignificance. She was able to reflect on the strangeness of that afterwards, and wonder at it, and the reason why it should be thus, but just then nothing else seemed important save one person. One man, who stood out from the rest like a live human being would against a grey cardboard background with shadows for people. He wore a pale blue open-necked shirt under a deeper blue pullover, the sleeves pulled up to his elbows. Tight blue jeans covered his long powerful legs, and he exuded an aura of strength and authority. No doubt about who was in charge. There could be no other one but him, and he knew it.

Then he turned away again, busily engrossed in his work. The moment passed. The gesture was dismissive. He didn't care if she was there or not. Jan made her way to the grassy bank and sat beside her sisters, and prepared to watch.

It was fascinating to see the team in action—and to watch her own father positively relishing the situation in which he found himself. There was a break after half an hour or so. Vacuum flasks were produced, and there was hot coffee for everyone, and Jan went over to her father who was standing with Dee. 'You are an odd old ham,' she said. Dee laughed, and Mr. Sutherland looked faintly bemused.

'I'm—er—not sure what you mean,' he said. But the corners of his mouth twitched, and Dee said:

'I think Jan means that you're doing so well you seem like a true professional.'

'Ah!' Her father nodded wisely. 'I see.'

'You're loving every minute of it,' Jan went on.

'Well, yes, I suppose I am,' he admitted. 'I never imagined it would be like this. Er—am I doing all right?'

'Splendidly, Mr. Sutherland,' then as Breck came near, Dee added: 'I was just telling Mr. Sutherland that you're pleased.'

'Indeed I am.' Breck smiled slightly at Jan's father. 'And what we'd like—when you've finished your coffee—is for one of your daughters to come over to you, as if calling you back for a meal. As they're here,' and he nodded vaguely towards Helen and Judy.

'Perhaps Jan——' Cedric Sutherland began, hesitantly.

'No,' said Jan. 'Not me. I'd rather not.' And she turned and walked away. She knew she was being childish and possibly rude, but she couldn't stay near Breck a moment longer.

She watched, all the same, from her vantage point with Helen as Judy was filmed running as if from the house, was taken standing briefly at the top of the rise before scrambling down to her father at the lochside.

'That's fine, Judy,' Breck called, and gave her the thumbs up sign. 'But just let's do it once more, okay?' He strode over to her and spoke quietly, his right arm going out, upwards, pointing. The cool professional who seemed to know exactly what he was doing—who could, as Terry had once said, get the best out of everybody. Judy listened intensely, nodding, smiling, eager to please.

Jan closed her eyes. First her father, now Judy, who had changed completely these last few days. She glanced discreetly at Helen who watched as avidly as anyone, hiding any disappointment she might feel very well. There's only me, she thought. I'm the odd one out. Perhaps there's something the matter with me.

Another hour passed, and they were nearly done for the day. Scudding clouds hid the sun, and Breck called: 'Okay, break for five minutes.'

Dee collapsed beside Jan with a sigh. 'Phew! Nearly over. It'll be good. Your dad is just fine, Jan. You get some people who tighten up when they see a camera, but not him. The way he handles that boat is super. He might even make a fortune when people see the film!'

'I doubt it,' Jan laughed. 'He keeps going on about how he'll invent something to revolutionize the world, but I think he's secretly happiest just pottering about here. He'd hate to be famous.'

'Lucky man,' said Dee. 'To know what you want to do—and do it, that's happiness.'

She made it sound easy. I wonder what I want, thought Jan. Life on Dark Isle had always been exactly what she wanted—until recently. Now she felt strangely restless, and unsure of herself. And when Dee got up to start work again she left her sisters and went back to Craigie House.

Tuesday began like any other day; Jan was up early to make herself a cup of coffee which she drank in the kitchen surrounded by peace and quiet before the usual bustle began. Her foot was so much better that she was back to normal with all household tasks. There was breakfast to prepare, for ten people and not just four, and she emptied her cup and went to switch on the grill ready for the bacon. All the crew had enormous appetites. They blamed it on the fresh sea air, but Jan privately considered that they had been just too busy in London to bother with food. Her mental picture of the capital of England was a place where everyone ate at cafés, or snatched sandwiches instead of having proper lunch.

'Hi!' Dee's voice interrupted her flow of thought as she laid rasher after rasher of bacon on the grill. 'Anything I can do?'

'Yes. Cut the bread, please—over there. Thanks, Dee. You're up early.'

'Mmm, I know. A tantalizing whiff of coffee floated up to my bedroom and woke me.'

'Help yourself. Coffee pot's on the table,' Jan laughed. 'What are you doing today?'

'Your dad's showing us how his telescope works. The one on the roof. It's not dangerous up there, is it? I'm terrified of heights.'

'No. There's a collapsible ladder from the attic up to a flat section of roof. It's nearly as big'—Jan frowned looking round her—'no, bigger than this kitchen, and there's a stone parapet, so it's quite safe. Anyway, you won't all have to be up there, will you?'

'Don't know. Still, I am curious, I must admit. Does he really study the stars?'

'Yes. You should see the moon through it some time. You can almost imagine you're going to spot one of those American flags, it's so detailed. He has another land telescope up there too. You can see for miles and *miles* on a clear day.'

Dee, busy cutting bread, pausing only occasionally for a swig of coffee, looked sceptical. 'Mmm, it sounds very interesting,' she managed at last.

Jan smiled. 'You don't mean it at all. I'll take you up after breakfast if you want. Before the crowd goes, and you can look round in peace for a few minutes, of course, you won't exactly see any stars, but I'd like to know what you think. You may come down converted.'

'You're on!' Dee giggled. 'I'd like to see *their* faces if I know all about how to use a telescope and they don't. Can we sneak off?'

'Easy. Leave it to me.'

It was simply a case of walking out with a few plates to the kitchen, leaving everyone else still at the breakfast table. They ran upstairs, and Jan opened the dusty attic and manipulated the ropes that pulled the aluminium ladder into place.

'Okay, shall I go first?' she asked Dee.

'Please do.' Dee looked wide-eyed as Jan mounted the ladder and pushed open the skylight, with an ease born of long experience. Jan leaned back to help Dee up the last few steps, and then the two girls stood on the flat roof, surrounded by chimneys and a low stone parapet.

'Over here,' Jan said, and led Dee over to the two telescopes which were covered with tarpaulin secured firmly to the roof with ropes threaded into huge metal rings.

'Careful now, this one is heavy to manoeuvre,' she warned her, touching the giant telescope with affection. 'Daddy will love this. He's only waiting for the night when he discovers a new star or something.' She left Dee studying the huge powerful instrument, and went over to the other, smaller one. It swung round easily, and Jan peered into the lens,

160

moving it slowly, scanning the area, focussing it as she did so, preparatory to finding an interesting view for Dee. Trees and hills sprang into life and colour, seemingly only feet away from her hand. No longer three-dimensional but flat, yet it was fascinating to see everything from this angle, and Jan forgot Dee in her absorption. She remembered the island and swung slowly round to the left to find it. Just a short boat ride away it was, and it had no name, but years ago, sheep had grazed there, and very occasionally they went over in the boat and had a picnic. Rocky outlines sprang to life, bushes and trees appeared clearly instead of a distant blur —and someone moved in the trees, and then disappeared. Jan blinked. Had she imagined it? No one ever went there now. The crofter who had grazed sheep there had died years ago. She swung the telescope downwards to scan the shore for signs of a boat, but there was nothing, only a pile of seaweed and driftwood with a gull atop it.

'Can I see?' asked Dee.

'Mm, yes. I was just finding a good view of another little island for you, and I thought I saw someone, but it must have been a shadow or something.' Jan stood aside to let Dee peer through the eye.

'What's it called?'

'The island with no name—that's what *we* call it, because it hasn't got one,' Jan answered.

'Logical enough, I suppose.' And Dee laughed, but Jan wasn't really listening. She was picturing the moving figure again, hidden by trees. Had it been a trick of the light? Possibly. Sunlight passing through branches could cause all sorts of shapes and movement. Better to forget it. And the next minute she did, as clattering footsteps up the ladder warned of the arrival of others.

'They're here,' she told the engrossed Dee. 'I'd better go and clear the breakfast things away.'

Her father came first, followed by Terry, and Breck and Tom.

Terry grinned at Jan. 'There are two men in your kitchen,' he said. 'Helping the girls. Just put the breakages on the bill.'

'I'm going anyway, Terry,' Jan smiled at him. 'See you later. I'll send up coffee in an hour or so.' And she left them to it.

By noon the sun had departed. One minute everything was bright, the next, heavy rain clouds swelled the sky, threatening to burst, and a darkness came over the island that was like the gloom before a storm—but there was no storm. Jan, working in the lounge, heard the wind howling down the chimney, and shivered. It was strange how suddenly everything had changed, and there would be no more outdoor filming done that day. Perhaps she had better light the fire in their working room for them.

Dee was the first to come down. 'Brr!' she shivered. 'It went suddenly cold and windy up there. Your dad says there'll be a storm.'

'I shouldn't be surprised.' Jan stood back and watched the wood catch alight and begin to crackle under the coal. 'That'll soon be going. I'll make coffee.'

'I'll help you.' They went into the kitchen, and had to switch on the light to see what they were doing. Judy and Helen flung themselves in at the back door, giggling and laughing, carrying bowls of raspberries from the garden.

'It's gone terribly *funny*,' Helen said. 'We came in before we got drenched. It's going to pour down soon.'

'I know. And there'll be a gale blowing too, before long.' Jan looked out of the window to where trees were bending already in the wind. It was a strange green light—eerie. She didn't know why she should suddenly feel afraid.

Everyone was drinking coffee when the knocks came at the front door, and the elderly woman who was Mrs. MacPhail's neighbour stood there in great distress, almost crying. Jan took her arm. 'Mrs. Monroe,' she said, aware of the door behind her opening. 'Come in.'

The woman held on to Jan. She was trembling, and almost incoherent as she tried to speak. Jan half turned. 'A cup of coffee—quick,' she said crisply—then realized Breck was standing there. Running feet towards the kitchen, Dee going for the drink; Breck came forward and took Mrs. Monroe's other arm, and his eyes met Jan's over the old woman's head. Only anxiety there, not enmity, for it was almost as if they knew something awful was coming.

'It's Mrs. MacPhail,' the old woman managed at last, as they led her into the warmth of the sitting room. 'I went in to see her just now—but she's not there. And I don't know where she can be at all.'

CHAPTER TEN

IT took a few minutes to get the story from her.
Time for her to recover from her long walk, to
hold a beaker of hot coffee and sip it gratefully, to
have her ancient mackintosh removed, and to sit
her by the fire on a comfortable chair.

Everyone was silent, watching her; waiting. Until Breck took charge.

'Tell us exactly what happened, Mrs. Monroe,'
he said, pulling up a footstool beside her and sitting on it. 'It may help us to find her more
quickly.'

The old woman was grateful to have matters
taken out of her hands, you could tell. The old
fingers gripping the beaker trembled still, but she
was calmer than when she had come in.

'Aye well, I was just going to see that she had her
lunch ready, as I do most mornings, but she was
not there. The fire was not lit, and there was a pan
of soup on the stove, but it was not switched on.'
She took a deep breath. 'And her mac is gone from
the door.'

Breck looked up at Terry. 'But does she ever go
out, Mrs. Monroe?' he asked.

'Ach, no! Where would she go? She is not fit.
Jan knows that right enough, do you not, Jan?'

There was a knot of fear in Jan's stomach, but
she forced herself to answer lightly. 'But maybe she
felt well enough to go for a little walk—and decided to go on the spur of the moment, without

telling you,'

'But why is she not back?'

'She may be home by now,' Breck said gently. 'Terry, go in the Land-Rover and see.' And as the old woman made as if to get up, he put a hand on her arm. 'No, you stay here and finish your drink. We'll take you home in a while.' He followed Terry to the door, and Jan caught the almost whispered words as Terry went out, spoken far too quietly for Mrs. Monroe to hear: 'And go through the house—and back garden, while you're there.' He half turned. 'Tom, go with him, in case.'

In case she had fallen, and one of them had to stay with her while the other returned for help, Jan realized. She felt almost ill.

That was the worst time, waiting for the Land-Rover to return. Not knowing. Just standing around, everyone trying to make conversation and not quite succeeding, because Mrs. MacPhail was their favourite of all the islanders they had filmed for the documentary.

They heard the engine, then Terry and Tom came in. Terry shook his head. 'No, nothing.'

'Right.' Breck looked at his watch. 'We've got the Land-Rover and the van. How many bikes have you, Jan?'

'There are four in the stables. But it's very windy——'

'We'll have to manage. Right—Terry, go and shout Helen and Judy. Tom, you can go in the van——' He had taken over completely, and there was no arguing with him. Not that anyone wanted to. They were all ready to do anything he said.

'Jan, can Mrs. Monroe stay here? It might be better——' he nodded towards the old woman, and

Jan said:

'Yes, of course. I'll get my father to come in.' Her name had not been mentioned by Breck in his instructions of who was going where. 'Who do I go with?'

'I want you to stay here, for when we find her. Can we bring her here?'

'Yes. You don't think——'

'I don't think anything, except that there's a gale starting up, and it's going to lash it down any time now, and when we find her she'll need a good warm and a drink.'

'Yes, Breck.'

Within five minutes they had gone. Jan put more coal on the fire and drew up a chair near to the old woman. 'It's a good job you came,' she said. 'They'll find her, you see. She'll not be far from home.' She tried so hard to make the words convincing, and succeeded, for Mrs. Monroe nodded.

'Aye, yes. T'will not be long. He is a good sensible man, that Breck. They'll find her—and I shall tell her off right enough for scaring me like that, I can tell you!'

'I'm sure you will.' But the knot of fear wouldn't go away. There was something else at the back of Jan's mind too, some nameless worry that she could not put into words. A memory of something that had happened...

She went into the kitchen to refill the old woman's beaker, and when she looked out of the window and saw the shadows dancing in the wild trees. she knew what it was.

The island with no name. Someone had been there that morning. Mrs. MacPhail? Impossible! Yet was it? It was also impossible that she should have left her little home without a word to her nearest neighbour. Unheard of, yet it was so. It had happened. And now the old lady of over ninety had disappeared without trace, on an island where rain and gales threatened and the ground underfoot would soon be a treacherous quagmire. She must be found, and soon. She *had* to be found. Or she might die.

Jan didn't know how long the others would be. She looked at her watch, but it had stopped. There was a casserole cooking in the oven, nearly ready, but nothing as trivial as lunch seemed to matter now. The bowl of raspberries waited on the table. They would have to wait a little longer. For Jan knew she had to go to the island now. She would not delay any longer.

She went in with the coffee for Mrs. Monroe, saw that she was nearly asleep and helped her to the comfortable settee. 'Listen,' she said. 'I'm going to look for Mrs. MacPhail—I think she may be on the island with no name. If you need anything, my father will be in his den. I won't be long, though. You'll be all right?'

'Yes, I will. Och, dear, I hope you find her. Away you go, and mind now, be careful, the water is not good today.'

'I'll be all right. I'll be back before the others, maybe. You have a little rest. There are biscuits and cake in the kitchen if you're hungry—go and help yourself.'

She felt faintly guilty at leaving the old lady, but she was better there than alone in her own home, just waiting and worrying. And she knew she would not be long ...

The water was indeed 'not good'. Jan sat in the

boat and started the outboard motor. A spare can of petrol rested reassuringly at her feet, and she had the oars. She would be there within minutes. The salty spray came up over the sides, and she folded the blanket more securely on her knees and pulled her warm anorak down over it. Underneath she had put on an extra jumper, because Mrs. MacPhail would be cold. In her pocket the medicine bottle she had filled with whisky chinked against a coin. She was by now positive that she would find the old woman there, and the main consideration was to keep her warm and comfortable. Even though Jan had no idea how she could have got there in the first place ...

The small boat was bucketed about, and then the rain began, lashing down with sudden fury as if resentful of anyone being foolish enough to dare the weather. Jan was used to the loch. She had been used to boats since childhood, and was a strong swimmer, but even she felt a twinge of unease as the outboard engine spluttered in a losing battle with a sea which grew wilder by the minute. Nearly there—thank heavens the island wasn't far away. Not far—but she seemed to be making no progress at all. Turning her head, she saw the craggy outline of the strip of land waiting for her. Where would she be? In the bothy? Or wandering about, perhaps forgetful of why she was there? She must be found, and quickly. Then they would return, if they were able. Jan had that tight knot of fear again, and now there were several reasons for it, but it spurred her on, to nurse the boat, willing the engine to do its best, and if thought could power the boat, she would be there already, so hard was she concentrating.

Unbelievably, she felt the scrape of the boat's keel against solid ground. She was there. Jumping out, wading the last few steps through shushy spray, Jan pulled the boat safely out of the water and as far up the beach as she was able. Now it was safe, and so was she.

'Mrs. MacPhail—Mrs. MacPhail!' The wind whipped the sounds away immediately they were uttered, and Jan began to run towards the bothy, for it was the most sensible place to shelter, and she would leave the blanket there before searching the rest of the island.

But the small shepherd's hut was empty and cold. Not even a mouse hid there. Jan stood in the doorway and looked round the tiny room, and it would be lovely just to sit down and go to sleep . . .

She put the blanket on the floor and, taking a deep breath, went out into the gathering storm. She knew every inch of the island, and if it took hours, she would search every spot where an old lady might fall, or shelter.

It didn't take that long. The trees were the first, obvious place, because it was there she had seen the someone she had thought must be Mrs. MacPhail. The leaves provided some protection from rain, but not from wind. Branches whipped against her, an ominous crack came from nearby and she swung round, ducking instinctively as a broken limb crashed awkwardly to the ground near her.

She called the name, and the howling wind took it up, mocking her cruelly, and Jan ran onwards, dodging twigs and stones, surefooted because of fear, forgetting her ankle, which was better anyway, and just as well . . .

Standing trembling inside the door of the bothy,

she knew at last that her journey had been in vain. There was no one else on the island with no name. Not another soul. Jan was alone. Before she set off home she would sit down for five minutes to regain her strength, for she would need it all if she were to make a safe journey back.

She sat on the folded blanket, remembered the whisky, and took a warming sip, setting the blood tingling again through cold numbed limbs. She put the bottle down beside her on the floor. She might have just one more sip, for courage, before she set off—and she saw the faded scrap of material on the dusty stone beside the whisky. She picked it up and shook it, to reveal a red spotted neck-scarf. It must have been there for years, for it was dry and dusty and creased. She put it down again. Breck's grandfather had worn a scarf like that sometimes in winter. How strange that after all these years, she should be the one to find it. He used to come to the island for herbs, and once, after his rescue, he had brought Jan with him for a treat, and she had helped him pick tiny yellow flowers ...and she had forgotten all about that, until this moment.

Jan put her head down on her arms and thought about Breck. The filming was nearly done. Soon he would leave. And life, which had changed so irrevocably, would somehow have to go on. Not as before. It could never be the same again. Not for Jan. She knew that now. Perhaps time would ease the pain. Perhaps ...

It was time to go. The longer she stayed, the more difficult it would be to leave, for the wind howled its eerie song down the chimney, and the rain rattled on roof and window in a relentless cascade that went on and on and on.

She was nearly knocked off her feet as she went out of the door. She began to run to the beach—and saw the wild sea, the white horses—and further out, huge swollen waves. Dark Isle had vanished completely, swallowed in blackness. Jan looked round her, and knew utter desolation. She could have been alone in the world. And now, as she turned and ran back to the bothy, she knew real, deep, overwhelming fear.

The wood crackled, bright yellow flames and red sparks shooting up the chimney, and filling the room with warmth and light. Jan's despair had not lasted long, nor the fear. She was safe, she had shelter, and all she had to do was stay right where she was until the storm died down, and then leave.

She had removed her soaking anorak and trousers and spread them in the hearth to dry. Wrapped in the blanket, she sat in front of the fire and ate the squashed bar of chocolate she had found in her anorak pocket. She firmly put out of her mind any wistful memories of the lovely hot casserole. That was negative thinking. She had chocolate, and that was sufficient. She had warmth, and soon her clothes would be dry, and the rain and gales would stop, and she would go. They would have found Mrs. MacPhail by now, and she should never have come, because if she had listened to common sense she would have known that the old woman was literally incapable of rowing a boat to an island. She hadn't stopped to think about it. Jan pondered on her stupidity, which, now she came to think about it, *really* think, had been monumental.

So why did I do it? she thought. There was no one to answer.

Breck would give her one of his long cool stares when she returned home. He wouldn't need to laugh at her—but it would be there, quite plainly, on his expressive face. I don't care, Jan thought. Let him think what he likes. I had to come, I just had to—even though I'm still not sure why.

The last piece of chocolate tempted her, but she put it on the mantelpiece. In a while she would have it, not now. Something to look forward to. She wriggled her toes in the thick socks she had donned before she left home. Soon her clothes would be dry, but the blanket was quite warm, and sitting like this, hands clasped round knees, in front of a good fire with a pile of wood in the corner that she and her sisters had found and left there on their last picnic, she was really quite comfortable. She hadn't imagined, when they had collected the driftwood and twigs, just how useful they would be, and when. She put her head forward and rested it on her knees...

Breck's grandfather was pulling her out of the water, scolding her gruffly, calling her name: 'Jan —Jan!' and she opened her eyes, because the dream was so real that it was almost painful, and saw the tall shadowy shape standing in the doorway. But she wasn't frightened. He'd returned for his scarf ... Then the shadow moved and came forward, and turned into Breck. Breck!

Shakily, still half asleep, Jan scrambled to her feet, and picked up the dusty scarf. 'I thought it was your grandfather calling——' she began.

Breck was soaking wet. The water dripped off him in streams as he stood there. 'You—you——'

172

he seemed incapable of speech, unusual for him, thought Jan, confused. She pulled the blanket round her more securely and went nearer him.

'Hadn't you better get your oilskin off?' she said. 'It's dripping all over the floor.'

'Is that *all* you can say?' His voice was husky, and if he wasn't angry he was making a good imitation of it. Jan quelled the instinctive rising temper that always let her down whenever he was within five yards. She looked quickly towards the window, but could see nothing. It was as black as night outside —and then she realized. 'It's terrible out,' she said. 'You came in this? I was waiting until it improved——' her voice tailed off as his face darkened.

'Yes, I did come in this—and yes, it was terrible. But I had no choice, had I?'

'I didn't ask you!' she retorted. 'I'm quite safe here——'

'And do you think we knew? Your family are going frantic——' he produced what looked like a stick of dynamite from under his oilskin. 'Stay *there*,' he said. 'I promised I'd let off this flare when I found you.' And he went out.

Jan let her breath out in a long slow sigh of relief. She scrambled into her dry trousers and put her wellingtons on again. Then, going to the corner, she pulled more sticks of wood from the pile and flung them on to the fire.

The door opened and he came in again, and undid the oilskin, leaving it by the doorway. 'Come and get warm by the fire,' Jan said. 'And there's some whisky——' she lifted the bottle up. 'Please have some,' she added. Because it was beginning to sink in now that she was fully awake, just precisely

173

how and why he had come.

'Oh, thank you so much,' the harsh sarcasm coloured her cheeks, but she bit back any retaliatory answer.

'I'm sorry I caused all this trouble. I thought Mrs. MacPhail was here. Have you found her?'

'Yes.' He swallowed a good portion of the whisky and handed the bottle back to her. 'She's at your house, and she's all right.'

Tears sprang to Jan's eyes. 'I'm so glad,' she whispered.

'Why the hell didn't you wait for us to return?' he demanded, moving nearer to the fire. Jan noticed that he was shivering. He crouched down and put his hands to the blaze. 'God, that's better.'

'I couldn't. I didn't know how long you'd be—or if you'd find her, and the weather was getting worse. Don't you *see*?'

'It still is—getting worse, I mean. And no, I don't see. Nobody in their right mind would expect an old woman of over ninety to come haring over to this deserted island.'

'Well, I did,' Jan said flatly. Why was it so difficult to keep her temper? But she would try. 'So perhaps I'm not in my right mind. Come to that, no one made you come after me, did they?'

He ignored that. 'Dee said something about you seeing someone here through the telescope—was that why?'

'Yes. And *you* wouldn't understand.'

He stood up, rubbing his hands together. 'That's a bit better. No, I wouldn't, so don't bother explaining. I don't think I can take too many explanations from you. I fight my way across in a boat that threatens to overturn every second—a very hairy experience, I might add—to be greeted by you with the words: "I thought it was your grandfather——"'

'I did. I must have been dreaming——'

'I'll bet you were! Just don't bother to tell me all about it. There's a limit to my patience.'

Jan's eyes blazed. 'I'm trying—I'm really *trying* not to get angry with you,' she said. 'But you make it very difficult. You are quite insufferable and extremely aggressive.'

'You'd make a saint have aggressive tendencies,' he grated.

'And you're far from being one,' she shot back. 'So why don't you just shut up? I was quite happy on my own.'

He reached inside his anorak and produced a large bulky package. 'Not hungry, then? Children are usually foul-tempered when their stomachs are empty. Your sisters made these while I was out commandeering a boat. Get them down you—it might improve your disposition.'

The temptation to fling them back at him was only overcome by her protesting stomach. Jan took the package and undid it to see a pile of squashed sandwiches. She thought she had never seen anything so utterly delicious. She swallowed. 'Do you want one?'

'I thought you'd never ask. No, thanks. They filled me up with hot soup and casserole before letting me go.'

She didn't care. She sat down and fell on the sandwiches. Cheese and tomato had never tasted quite as exquisite before. But even so, she left three, which she carefully wrapped again and put on the stone mantelshelf. It was true, she did feel much better. She even managed to look up at him and say:

'Thank you.'

'A pleasure. And you've got tomato pips on your chin—if you're interested.'

She wiped her chin on her pullover sleeve. Breck sat down beside her.

'Want a cigarette?'

'No, thanks.' She knew a sudden wave of utter weariness. What was the use? Everything she said or did was wrong, she knew that. There was no way to change the situation, it was too late, much too late. She put her head forward and rested it on her knees, and Breck said:

'Don't you feel well?'

'Yes. I'm just tired, that's all.' And not far from tears, but she wouldn't tell him that. 'Can we leave soon?'

'I doubt it. Are you joking?'

'No.' She looked at him. 'I thought that was why you came, to take me—back——' she faltered. Why was he staring at her like that?

'I've got news for you. It's nearly six—and can you hear the wind? Look at the smoke—try and look out of the window, but you'll not see a thing. It's getting worse. We're in for a hell of a storm—let's hope this bothy is made of good stuff, because this is where we're staying. This is the one safe place on this island—and so this is where we remain until the wind and rain die down. And that could be in the morning.'

The words didn't register at first. Then they did. In quite a small voice, Jan said: 'We're going to have to stay here all night, aren't we?'

'Why yes, I do believe we are!' he sounded

faintly surprised, as if she had made a startling pronouncement. 'How clever of you!'

'There's no need to be sarcastic.'

'I try, believe me I try, but it's difficult. Do you have to make such stupid remarks?'

'Oh!' She scrambled to her feet and went to the door. It was nearly wrenched out of her hand as she opened it, and the wind blasted in, sending rain spattering at her feet. To step out in that would be to be soaked in an instant. Breathlessly she tried to slam the door shut, but the wind force was too strong. Breck strode over with a muttered oath, grabbed the handle and slammed the door shut. The catch clicked home. He looked down at her. 'Going out for a walk—or are you satisfied now?'

She turned away without answering, and he grabbed her arm and swung her round. 'Well, are you?'

'Yes.'

'Good. So now perhaps you'll accept the fact that we're stuck here—not by choice, but nevertheless, here we are and here we'll stay until it's safe to leave. And there's nothing you can do about it.'

'I don't have to stay here!' she said desperately, foolishly.

'Yes, you do. I'm not chasing all over the damned island looking for *you*.'

'Let go of my arm. I'd rather sit in a tree all night than sit looking at *you*,' she retorted. 'You're an absolute bully!'

He laughed. She wondered what dreadful consequences would result if she hit him—but she already knew. 'With you I am. God help the man you marry! I only hope he has the sense to give you the beating you deserve occasionally——'

She wrenched her arm free. 'You talk big, *Mister* Breck Fallon, really big—but one of these days you'll meet someone stronger than you, and I hope I'm there to see it. And the man I marry is my business. One thing—I'll make certain he's not a bit like you, that's for sure!'

'I'll bet you will. It's not a man you want, it's a lapdog,' he grated.

It was Jan's turn to laugh. 'Heavens, you call yourself a man?' she taunted. 'The only way you ever get a kiss is by *force*. I feel sorry for you.' And she turned her back on him deliberately.

There was an electric moment of silence. She knew she had gone too far, but a reckless temper drove her on. From the safe distance of the window, she said: 'And you're not so good at that either.'

It was all blackness outside, and the room was reflected in the glass, so that she saw him move, knew he was coming over to her, and braced herself instinctively. And then the light from the fire was blotted out by his shadow, and he was behind her, moving in, putting his hands on her shoulders as distantly, she heard the howling of the wind, a faint lightning flash to light the sky with electric blue, and her back stiffened in fear, all nerve ends a-tingle as he said softly:

'You're a little liar—but let's see what this one does, shall we?' and she was being swung round. It was as though it was happening in slow motion, blurred, like an old film, out of focus, the sounds of the storm coming nearer and nearer, matching the explosiveness in that small room as Breck took her in his arms and kissed her, hard and brutally. A thousand stars shattered; she thought that lightning had struck the room. The primitive, savage response frightened Jan as she fought for her freedom from this man, whose strength was twice that of any normal man. Then, with a cry, she freed herself and ran from him, across the room, trembling, realizing the deep truth within her...

She wrenched the door open, ignoring his shouted command, feeling the rain deluging down, cleansing the memory of that kiss away, soaking her to her skin instantly—and she went reckless into the darkness and the gale which tried to pull her off her feet. But it was preferable to him—and if she could reach the boat—if only she could reach it ... Trees swayed and creaked, even above the howling wind, and she heard her name faintly called, and a sob was wrenched from her throat as she ran and stumbled, falling once, getting to her feet again, the tears washed away by rain, mingling with it, blinding her anyway so that she saw nothing. But she heard the crash of thunder at the same moment that the whole world was lit up with the most devastating flash of lightning. The ground shook, the huge tree in her path toppled slowly forward, and she heard Breck's voice, not distantly now, but closer, much closer—coming nearer every second. Then she was yanked violently off her feet as the tree crashed down in the path, only feet in front of her—where she would have been, if Breck hadn't pulled her to him, if he wasn't holding her, picking her up, carrying her back to the bothy. But why did he tremble so? She did not know. Perhaps he wasn't as strong as she thought...

He put her down in the bothy, and then he slammed the door shut, and Jan, still recovering from the shock, looked at him, and saw how white he had gone.

'I was going to the boat,' she blurted out.

'I know.' He was drenched too, although he had stopped to put the oilskin on. He took it off. 'You'd better get your clothes off—you'll get pneumonia.'

'Then you'd be rid of me—so why are you concerned?'

'Jan, don't argue. Just do it. I'll turn away. Your anorak's dry—you can dress in that, and the blanket. Do it now.'

She was shivering violently, and could scarcely strip off her wringing wet pullover, so clinging was it. But she managed, and quickly zipped up her anorak over her bra. The blanket made a long skirt, and was secure enough tucked inside the anorak. She spread out the trousers and jumper in the hearth to dry, and Breck said: 'Ready?'

'Yes.' She crouched down. Despair filled her. This was it. The next few hours would pass, and the storm would die away—but she couldn't take much more from Breck. And when he moved and sat down beside her, she withdrew, huddled as small as possible, like a child fearing attack, waiting for the anger, the explosive temper that would inevitably follow her stupid and reckless escape bid.

'All right, Jan, the fight is over. It's no use. We can't go on like this,' he said, and she saw that he was still pale, even in the firelight, the flickering gold from the branches that burned erratically and cast their glow around them. She dared a swift sidelong glance at him, unsure if she was imagining his words. Where was the aggression, the hard arrogance? It was not there now. He spoke quietly, almost tiredly.

Jan put her hand to her forehead to wipe away a trickle of water that escaped from her hair, which was still soaking, and she shivered, suddenly very cold and wanting comfort. And Breck reached out to touch her hair, softly, gently.

'We must get that dry,' he said. 'Lean forward.' Jan obeyed because it was easier to do that than to resist him. Then, after a pause, he was rubbing her hair. But with what? There was no towel there. She put up her hand, and he said: 'It's the scarf you found. It's all right, I've shaken it. It will get the worst off.'

'Leave me—I'll do it.' She was weary, so very weary.

'No. More forward—that's it.' And he put his hand on the back of her neck to move her head slightly. Only then he wasn't taking it away, as he should have, and that touch became warm; a caress almost, as he said: 'Jan, oh, Jan, what are we doing to each other?'

She lifted her head slightly, moved it gently from side to side, revelling in his touch. Tingling, filled with warmth it was, and strength. She could feel that strength flowing from him to her, giving her the infinite courage to say:

'I don't know, Breck—I don't know——'

And suddenly the words didn't matter any more as he enfolded her in his arms, and now he was kissing her as never before. Nothing brutal—but tenderly, beautifully, wonderingly...

'Oh, Jan,' he murmured huskily, 'It's no use at all. Absolutely no use. You are the most maddening, infuriating, provoking woman I've ever met in my life, and because of you, I found out for the first time ever what real suffering was today.'

He was making no sense at all, but it didn't matter, because something else was coming across to her now, and in a way that was utterly delicious, warm, and comforting. 'I don't know what you mean,' she murmured, but she was beginning to, very slowly.

'I found out what hell was like when they told me you'd vanished in a little boat to the island with no name. Don't you *see*? Don't you *know*?'

'And you came after me,' she said.

'Of course I came after you. I had no choice, had I?' He groaned suddenly and pulled her towards him even more closely, which was almost impossible, but he managed it. 'Because I found out that I loved you, dammit.'

'Oh,' she said.

'Is that *all* you can say?'

'Yes, it is.'

'Well, that's a change. And at least you're not laughing. That's something else to be thankful for, I suppose. Why aren't you laughing?'

'Because I don't feel like it. We're not going to have another fight, are we?'

'No. Sorry to disappoint you, love, but you just knocked all the fight out of me.'

She looked at him, her eyes darker and soft. 'You won't be the same man,' she said mischievously— happily. And there must have shown something in her face, for he drew in his breath sharply.

'Jan?'

'Yes?' Very softly. Then, repeated: 'Yes, love?'

'Ah!' And now he sighed. 'So Terry was right!'

'What?' She was puzzled.

He squeezed her tightly. 'My assistant told me, in an outburst of frankness, that I couldn't see what

was going on under my nose, and that I was a fool
—among other things—and I'd have undoubtedly
fired him except that he's too clever—and besides,
he spoke the truth, didn't he?'

'I don't know what he said, do I?'

'He said that it was quite obvious to the world at
large that we were suffering with the pangs of love
for each other, and that the only two people who
weren't aware of it was us.'

'Oh, I see.' Jan swallowed hard.

'So I'll have to promote him instead, won't I?'

'It looks like it.'

'And he'll have to be best man.'

'But—er—what *at*?' she asked, with scant regard
for grammar.

'What do you think? A wedding. Yours and
mine. I can't live without you, I know that. Will
you? Marry me, I mean?'

'But we—I mean, yes, I love you, and I can't imagine life without you, but—we're always fighting,
aren't we?' she finished.

'Who knows? We may even learn to become
friends. At least life will never be dull. I don't care
where we live. I'll learn to grow vegetables and
things, and fish and mow the lawn——'

'You mean you'd stay *here*, on Dark Isle?'

'With you—yes.'

'Oh, *Breck*.' It had all been dreamlike so far, because it had all happened so suddenly that she had
had no time to think. But now it was real and wonderful, absolutely wonderful. 'That's not right. I
couldn't expect that. I don't believe what's happening—but I'm beginning to—and I know that
my place would be wherever you wanted to be.'

'Right, that's settled. We'll have six months here

and six months in London every year.' He began to laugh. 'We're both mad, you know that? Talking about our future life together, and we barely know each other. And you know something else? I don't care. I know it's right. You know, when I came here I was filled with bitterness towards my grandparents because they had turfed my mother out because she wanted to be a doctor. They didn't believe in women having a career. She had to struggle, manage on her grant and work damned hard every moment she could spare—and they cut her from their lives completely. She's never got over it, and I intended making this docuumentary to show just how narrow and bigoted—and cruel—people could be. In a way they were, of course, but all my bitterness has gone,' he paused to stir the fire with a twig, sending sparks flying upwards to vanish. 'Because all the people here, Mrs. MacPhail, the others, have helped me see things in a different light. I'll be able to go and tell my mother a lot of things that will help both of us to see everything differently. Plus one important fact, more important than anything else.' He looked at Jan softly, and she said:

'What is that?'

'The fact that my grandfather saved your life. Nothing matters more than that. I would forgive him everything, because without him being there at that special moment, I wouldn't have had you, my own love.'

'Oh, Breck!' Jan blinked back tears. 'Thank you for telling me. I knew something awful had happened in the past. I'm sorry, love. But I did like your grandfather. He became far more human somehow after that day. I came here with him once, looking for plants.' And she stopped, because she was seeing something again in her mind's eye, something from years ago—and again from this morning.

'What is it, Jan?'

'It's just—oh, this will sound so stupid. It's too silly for words, but—that figure I saw in the trees this morning, it was very vague and shadowy. It could have been anything—or nothing. But it could have been—*him.*'

'You mean my grandfather—or rather his ghost?' He began to smile.

'I *know,*' Jan persisted. 'I said it was silly, but——'

'There are no such things, my love, and anyway, it was only because Mrs. MacPhail went missing that you——' and then his voice tailed away, and his expression changed.

'What is it?' gasped Jan.

He shook his head. 'No! You're getting me at it now. This is ridiculous!'

'What *is it?*' she repeated fiercely, and Breck laughed.

'All right, you scare me when you look like that!' Well, when we found the old lady she said——' he paused.

'Go *on,*' Jan urged.

'She said that she had had the sudden compulsion to go and pick raspberries this morning, something she'd not done for years and years, and the desire had been so overwhelming that she'd just got out of her chair and gone—and she didn't know *why,* because she didn't even like them particularly——'

'I know she doesn't,' Jan began to laugh quietly.

'Oh, Breck, now do you believe me!'

'No! Anyway, there she was, she said, busily picking away, and quite enjoying herself, apparently, when the weather had suddenly changed and she'd taken shelter in an old croft. That was where we found her, quite safe, but a little tired and cold. She'll be fine now. Dee was making her soup when I left—assisted by Terry, I hasten to add, and surrounding her with blankets and hot water bottles.' He turned to Jan and gently kissed her cheek. 'Okay, if it makes you happy, it was my grandfather who made you come here,' and he looked upwards. 'Thanks, Granddad!'

'You're an idiot,' Jan murmured, but she didn't mean it. And he knew that.

'Oh, love,' he said, 'I'll never hurt you again, like I have done. How could I have been such a brute? That first time we met, on the road—when I nearly managed to run you over, I knew something then—hadn't a clue what it was, but there was this tingle, a spark if you like, and subconsciously I had the urge to let you see I wouldn't have a slip of a girl like *you* bossing me——'

'You told me. You threatened to tame me, if I remember rightly.'

He groaned. 'So I did too. What a memory you possess!'

'Mmm, yes, I do.'

'It didn't quite work out according to plan, did it? You tamed me. What a girl!'

Jan moved more comfortably in his warm embrace. 'Breck,' she began, 'about where we'll live, I'll come to London if you like—I can't let you sacrifice your work——'

'Ah, yes. Well, there's something I forgot to tell

186

you. I'm not only a producer with the TV company, I'm also one of the shareholders. I can please myself, my love, where I live and work. And somehow this place appeals more and more each day. I can go fishing while you write your book—then I'll turn it into a play and get Terry to produce it for you——'

'Stop!' she protested. '*Please*. I can't take all this in. Not all at once. Say it more slowly.'

'All right, I will. Ready? I told you that my father and mother are doctors, didn't I? Well, it's true. But Dad isn't a G.P. He's a consultant surgeon in a large London teaching hospital, as was his father before him, and my grandfather left me some money when he died. Enough to enable me to lead a life of leisure, which didn't appeal at all, so I put the money into shares in independent television, got myself a job twelve years ago on the ground floor, and worked my way up. No one knows—not even Terry—about the money. They just accept the fact that I like work—they don't know I have a personal interest in making damn good programmes, and that's the way I want it to stay. Only you know, because I'll tell you anything, my love.'

'Oh, Breck,' Jan knew she had to explain a certain something. 'You know how I was about television?'

'Ah, yes! Do I not? You're going to tell me it's all off, because you don't approve of my way of life? Fire away.' But he was smiling.

'No, please listen. Well, I——' she swallowed. 'You've converted me. I never thought I'd say it, but—well, you have.'

'Of course! What else? I told you I'd tame you,

didn't I? All right——' this as she moved threateningly, 'I was only joking. Honestly! Come here, woman—I'll show you who's the boss around here——' and after that, for quite a while, there was silence. Outside the storm went its course, gradually dying down, leaving only the rain spattering on the window of the bothy on the island with no name.

THE OMNIBUS
Has Arrived!

A GREAT NEW IDEA
From HARLEQUIN

OMNIBUS

The 3-in-1 HARLEQUIN — only $1.75 per volume

Here is a great new exciting idea from Harlequin. THREE GREAT ROMANCES — complete and unabridged — BY THE SAME AUTHOR — in one deluxe paperback volume — for the unbelievably low price of only $1.75 per volume.

We have chosen some of the finest works of world-famous authors and reprinted them in the 3-in-1 Omnibus. Almost 600 pages of pure entertainment for just $1.75. A TRULY "JUMBO" READ!

The following pages list some of the exciting novels in this series.

Climb aboard the Harlequin Omnibus now! The coupon below is provided for your convenience in ordering.

HARLEQUIN OMNIBUS

THE 3-IN-1 VOLUME — EACH BY THE SAME
AUTHOR — EACH ONLY $1.75

HARLEQUIN OMNIBUS

THE 3-IN-1 VOLUME — EACH BY THE SAME
AUTHOR — EACH ONLY $1.75